All of London is abuzz with stories of the beautiful Royle sisters. Could these slightly scandalous triplets truly be the "secret" daughters of the highest prince in the land? One of them has already done very well for herself by marrying a duke. Now Anne Royle is about to take center stage as she discovers. . .

HOW TO ENGAGE AN EARL

The last thing the Earl of MacLaren wants is a wife, so when he awakens to discover a fair-haired enchantress at the foot of his bed, he behaves as any man might, by taking full advantage of the delicious situation. Then his family bursts in, and the chit brazenly announces that she is his betrothed, so he finds himself well on his way to being leg-shackled for life!

Beautiful, reserved Anne Royle had never done anything so mad in her life. She entered the earl's bedchamber with no intention of seduction. Rather, she hoped to discover a document that could contain the truth about her heritage. But now her world is turned upside down, and while she trembles at the thought of her wedding night, she finds she longs for it in ways she never thought possible.

By Kathryn Caskie

HOW TO ENGAGE AN EARL
HOW TO SEDUCE A DUKE

Coming Soon

HOW TO PROPOSE TO A PRINCE

*If You've Enjoyed This Book,
Be Sure to Read These Other*
AVON ROMANTIC TREASURES

AND THEN HE KISSED HER *by Laura Lee Guhrke*
CLAIMING THE COURTESAN *by Anna Campbell*
THE DUKE'S INDISCRETION *by Adele Ashworth*
TWO WEEKS WITH A STRANGER *by Debra Mullins*
THE VISCOUNT IN HER BEDROOM *by Gayle Callan*

Coming Soon

BEWITCHING THE HIGHLANDER *by Lois Greiman*

Kathryn Caskie

How To Engage An Earl

An Avon Romantic Treasure

AVON BOOKS
An Imprint of HarperCollinsPublishers

For my grandmother Ivaloo,
whose passion in researching
the branches of our family tree
helped inspire this story.

AVON BOOKS
An Imprint of HarperCollins*Publishers*
10 East 53rd Street
New York, New York 10022-5299

Copyright © 2007 by Kathryn Caskie
Excerpt from *How to Propose to a Prince* copyright © 2008 by Kathryn Caskie
ISBN: 978-0-06-112484-6
ISBN-10: 0-06-112484-2
www.avonromance.com

First Avon Books paperback printing: July 2007

Avon Trademark Reg. U.S. Pat. Off. and in Other Countries, Marca Registrada, Hecho en U.S.A.
HarperCollins® is a trademark of HarperCollins Publishers.

Printed in the U.S.A.

10 9 8 7 6 5 4 3 2 1

Acknowledgments

I want to thank those people who helped see this story to completion, and whose contributions to the book, my career, and my writing life make this process so rewarding:

Lucia Macro, my wonderful editor, and Esi Sogah, who cleared their desks to make sure this book made it into production before the confetti was cleared from Times Square.

Jenny Bent, my fabulous agent at Trident Media Group, for always being there. You are the best agent a girl could have. As well as her dedicated assistant, Victoria Horn, for always looking out for me.

Franzeca Drouin, my very patient researcher, who always knows exactly where to find sources for even the most remote and bizarre historical details.

Nancy Mayer, Regency expert extraordinaire,

Kathryn Caskie

who went the extra mile to check the composition of period page cutters for me and to help me determine the requirements for a peer to take his family seat in the House of Lords. Your knowledge of the Regency period is invaluable to me.

My dear reader Peg, who trekked down to Cockspur Street and St. George's in London to gather some research materials for me.

Sophia Nash, friend and talented author, for her constant words of encouragement and for nudging me toward "the end" with the lure of shopping.

And finally, my eternal gratitude goes out to the makers of Red Bull (Sugar Free) and the baristas at Starbucks for keeping me sufficiently caffeinated during the course of writing this story.

Chapter 1

How to Become Invisible

Berkeley Square, London
April 1815

Unlike her far more vibrant sisters, Miss Anne Royle had but one talent—and it wasn't one to recommend her.

She could become invisible.

Oh, not in the way of fairy tales, where one's form could magically spread upon the breeze.

No, her talent was much more subtle than that.

Anne simply had the ability to move about a bustling drawing room *completely* unnoticed.

She considered herself naught but a specter in London society, and rightly so. After all, no one ever sought out her company, or tried to catch her eye. She could stand directly in front of a grand lord or lady, or even a tray-bearing footman, and more likely than not, she wouldn't be noticed.

Sometimes it was as if she simply did not exist.

Anne usually viewed her reputed *talent* as the darkest of damning curses.

But not always.

Only a year ago, she and her sisters, Mary and Elizabeth, had shed their black bombazine mourning frocks and left their tiny village in Cornwall for the satin elegance of London's drawing rooms.

Their effervescent sponsor, Lady Upperton, in her zeal to see the sisters properly matched, had mandated their attendance at an endless ribbon of unnerving balls, routs, and musicales.

Anne was no fool. Immediately she realized the benefit of moving beneath the raised noses of the *ton*.

It freed her from much of the scrutiny and whispers her sisters endured due to scandalous suspicions swirling about the Royle triplets' royal parentage.

And tonight would be no different.

As she and her sister Elizabeth primped and dressed in preparation for the grandest society rout in recent history, Anne actually prayed for invisibility.

For within five hours' time, the course of her life, and her sisters', would depend upon it.

MacLaren House, Cockspur Street
Three hours later

"Oh, Anne, how you exaggerate." Elizabeth laughed and swooshed her frilly lace-edged fan through the air, waving off the claim as if it were a bite-minded winged insect.

"I tell you, I can walk through this very crowd and eavesdrop on even the most private of conversations. No one will notice me. *No one.*"

"Can you now?" Elizabeth arched a dubious eyebrow at that. "And no one will see you?"

"*No one.*"

"Pish, posh. While your stealth is truly miraculous, you are hardly beneath notice."

Anne exhaled a long breath. Why did she even bother to try to explain it to Elizabeth? The

3

flame-haired beauty would never really understand the truth of it. How could she?

The reality of Anne's gift was that she was rather plain, at least in comparison to her sisters. For what else could explain her unnatural ability?

Physically, she should have stood out among the petite ladies of the *ton*. She was as tall as most men, after all. Still, she hadn't been blessed with rich sable hair like the eldest of the triplets, Mary, or the glossy copper locks of her sister Elizabeth, who had followed Anne into this world several minutes later.

No, the hair crowning Anne's head in a mass of tumbling ringlets was the shade of flax, so pale that it was nearly absent of color.

Even her features were delicate and unremarkable, and her skin was as white as a polished ivory tusk.

Sometimes Anne mused that if she stood against a wall wearing the very cream-hued gown she had donned this evening, no one would see her. Her coloring would make her virtually indistinguishable from the plaster.

Hmm. She might even test that theory. Why, who knew? With the feat she would attempt in

4

just two rounds of the minute hand, a new trick might be her saving grace in the event a quick escape was required.

In fact, it might be prudent to exercise her skills of stealth right this very moment, before . . . well, before she was called to action. Yes, that was exactly what she would do.

"Elizabeth, I vow, this very moment I could glide through this drawing room removing filled crystals of cordials from the fingers of unsuspecting guests, then leave them all wondering a moment later what had happened to them."

"No, you can't. You are merely having me on. I know you, Anne. But you must realize I am no longer your gullible, wide-eyed baby sister." Elizabeth chuckled into her hand.

"Still you doubt me. When will you ever learn, dear sister?" Anne caught up Elizabeth's gloved fingers and slapped her own fan into them. "I'll need both hands free. Now watch, my doubting miss . . . and be utterly amazed."

Laird Allan, the newly-belted Earl of MacLaren, opened the French windows, clapped a palm to his lady friend's round bottom, and firmly guided her into the dark passage.

Only one flickering candlestick glowed in the back hallway, and that was for the navigational sake of the additional staff engaged especially for tonight's rout. But the dimness just here suited Laird quite well.

"When may I see you again, Lady . . . er . . . my good lady?"

"Heavens, MacLaren, you don't even know my name, do you?" His lady friend straightened her frothy capped sleeves upon her smooth shoulders, then cupped her blushing full breasts and unashamedly readjusted their position inside her gown before looking up at him.

He raised his eyebrows and gave her a flat smile, to which she immediately responded with an overdone pout.

Laird sighed, in an equally false manner. "Please know, dear lady, my grasp of your name has nothing to do with how memorable you are. I am merely too deep in my cups to be able to retrieve it from my foggy mind, though I have no doubt your name is as lovely as you are. You'll forgive me. Won't you?"

She chuckled at that. "Now, now, do not fret, my handsome playmate." Reaching up, she pinched his cheek affectionately, then grinned.

"Truth be told, I am not offended in the least. In fact, darling, I am rather relieved. If you cannot remember my name, 'tis less likely that my husband will learn of our . . . intimate little tour of your garden during tonight's rout, eh?"

"You're married?" *Bloody hell. That makes two this night. Where are all the unattached misses? Still avoiding me like the pox? I've reformed. Or at least I'm trying. Married. Damn it.* He reached out his fingers and absently plucked a sprig of white-veined ivy from the woman's tumbling coiffure.

"Oh, you did not know?" A small laugh sailed upon her exhalation. "Never you mind. His aim is quite pitiful, I assure you. And he is dreadfully old, while you . . . well, you, my very virile earl, are not. Besides, you have yet to show me the moon garden. It is all that the ladies have been discussing this evening."

Doubtful, Laird raised a single eyebrow. "They are chatting about . . . the moon garden?"

"Oh yes. I daresay I was told, just an hour earlier, that that particular portion of the garden was most intoxicating . . . especially in the light of a full moon. Is that true, my lord?"

He held the sprig of ivy up to her and twirled

7

the leaf by its stem between his fingers. "You saw the garden, madam."

"But not *all* of it." She snaked a single finger seductively down his chest, stopping just above the waistband of his breeches. "And I would so enjoy seeing it all. Especially the moon garden." Her gaze bounced low in the event, he suspected, his foggy mind did not comprehend her barely veiled meaning. "Perhaps tomorrow evening you will show it to me, hmm?"

Laird cleared his throat. "I do apologize, but you must excuse me, madam. I really must rejoin my guests."

Her hand dropped lower, and she brazenly slid her fingers up his inner thigh as she leaned close and pressed a hard, wet kiss to his mouth. She playfully fumbled at one of the buttons closing his front fall. "Are you certain, my lord?"

Laird swiveled before her fingers could inflate matters. "I-I am afraid so, my dear. Must go."

"Truly?" She brought her lips to his ear, and her hardening words rode a heated breath. "Or could it be that you no longer have any more time for *me*, MacLaren. Is that it? I happen to know I was not the first to be led down your garden path tonight, and I daresay probably not the last, either." She nipped the pad of his earlobe.

Laird winced. Raising his hands between them, he caught her shoulders and held her in place as he took a step back.

"Well, if that is the way of it." She shot him a sharp, knowing glance, then turned on her scarlet Turkish heels and strode up the long passage toward the bright light streaming from the noisy drawing room.

Married. Laird shook his head in disgust. He'd tried so hard to put his rakish ways behind him for the good of the family. To show himself worthy, at last, of the MacLaren name . . . *and of her*.

For more than a year now, he'd been entirely respectable . . . as would be expected of a newly belted earl. His manners had been impeccable and his behavior nothing less than gentlemanly—that is, until tonight, anyway.

One night back in society. That's all it took. One night and he was already slipping back into his old unscrupulous ways. He shook his head. *Damn it all.*

But at least luck was with him. After all, Lady Goodsport, or whatever her name was, had made his push-off quite effortless.

Laird sighed as he lifted the candlestick and raised it to the mirror above the hall table to illuminate his face.

Just look at me—a bloody rumpled mess.

Then something about his blinking image pinched at him, and made him draw closer. His cobalt-hued eyes were cold and black in the dim reflection, and at once thoughts of his late father sprang unnervingly into his mind. He squeezed his eyes shut and drew in a deep breath, shaking off, as best he could, the image and the memories that trailed behind.

When he opened his lids again, Laird shoved his fingers through his wavy ebony hair, smoothing it into place. Turning away from the mirror, he deposited the candlestick on the cherry tabletop and set about attempting to retie the knot of his newly wrinkled neck cloth.

"You have a whole bloody house, MacLaren," came a low male voice from several feet up the passage.

Laird yanked his head around and squinted. Against the golden light breaking through the drawing room doors, he saw the familiar silhouette of a lanky gentleman.

"And yet tonight you prefer the garden," the man said.

"*Apsley.*" Laird turned fully, if a bit unsteadily, to face his old friend. "Sod me. Where have you been all night? Thought you'd changed your mind about coming and decided to take a turn with that saucy opera dancer of yours instead."

"Ah, well, no chance of that. Put that little minx on the shelf Tuesday." Apsley stole an admiring glance at himself in the mirror, tucking a stray curl back behind his ear.

Laird shook his head. "No doubt for another bit of muslin twice as . . . talented."

"Well, yes, if you must know." Arthur Fallon, Viscount Apsley, ruffled his blond locks and cockily tugged the points of his shirt collar higher, then turned again to face Laird. "But you had to have known I would come. I have not forgotten. Had he not . . . well, damn it, we'd be toasting your little brother's twenty-fifth birthday this night . . . instead of his memory."

Laird gazed down at the golden signet ring, all that had been returned to him a year ago by Graham's teary-eyed batman after the fateful battle that had taken his brother's life. "I miss him."

"I know. But you have to know, no matter what your father believed, it wasn't your fault. You have to understand that."

"It was, though. Had I done what Father had wished of me, Graham might not be dead." Laird leaned his head back while he blinked away the ridiculous tears of weakness stinging the backs of his eyes.

Apsley squeezed Laird's shoulder. "No more lamenting what may or may not have been." Then, like a hound catching a scent, he sniffed the air between them. "So brandy is your choice tonight, eh? Any good? I do hope it is, because I fear you might have a slight lead this eve. Can't have that, now can we?"

"More than a lead. My horse is lengths ahead, good fellow." When he looked up again, moisture pushed into his eyes. He raised the back of his hand to his face, to preserve his dignity, but the movement of his head, slight though it was, sent him staggering two steps to the left.

Apsley caught Laird's arm and steadied him. "So I see. But you shan't drink to Graham's memory alone for a moment longer." The corners of Apsley's lips turned upward. "Show me the decanter and your deepest crystal. I vow my horse will overtake yours within the hour!"

Laird smiled, knowing Apsley was quite serious, and all too capable. Before he could even think to oblige, he noticed they were no longer alone.

"Laird, son, that is you down there, is it not?" came Countess MacLaren's booming words from the far end of the long passage. "And is that Apsley's voice I am hearing as well? Is he with you?"

Oh good God.

Laird winced. "Yes, Apsley is here, Mother." Laird stepped forward and clapped his hand to the other man's arm, and then leaned close to speak quietly into his ear. "I do apologize, but I must warn you. My mother has been asking after you for hours."

"Has she?" Apsley held his words to a low whisper. "Oh bugger it, whatever for?"

The countess clapped her hands, and both men looked in her direction once more.

"We have guests who have just arrived. Please return at once and greet them. You are the head of the family now. They expect to see you," the countess hissed, before frantically dashing back into the drawing room.

Apsley's eyebrows lifted until they nearly grazed the golden lock of hair dangling over his forehead. "In a bit of a fluster, is she? So, tell me, Mac, what does the countess require of me this time?"

"The answer is quite amusing, really." Laird glanced toward the light and hastened his warning to Apsley, for certainly the countess would return to the passage within a moment's time.

"So tell me. I could use a bit of folly just now."

"If you can imagine it, it seems she is convinced you have enough sway to nudge me into my family's seat in the House of Lords."

Apsley laughed. "How you do go on."

"No, no, there is *more*." He raised a hand before the other man could interrupt again. "She even believes you possess the influence to urge me into marriage before the end of the season. Now, agreeing to abandon my profligate ways is one matter—but the parson's mousetrap? Ha! After what happened with Constance, I will never consider such lunacy again."

"Marriage, you say?"

Laird forced a laugh. "Isn't that diverting? As if anyone could ever convince me to become leg-shackled willingly again." He raised his eyebrows and waited for Apsley to do the same.

But he didn't.

Instead Apsley stared back at Laird as though he . . . as though he . . . *no*, surely he did not agree with her!

But Apsley was actually smiling.

Bloody hell, it seemed that he did agree.

"And you mock your mother's well-placed faith in me, sir? I assure you, I can be quite persuasive when I am passionate about something."

"That is true enough, except I happen to know you aren't invested in this cause, Apsley. Not in the least."

"Care to wager on it?" Apsley lifted his left eyebrow.

"Do yourself a good deed, save your guineas and a trip to White's to mark the book. For this would be one wager I would certainly win."

"Really?" Both of Apsley's eyebrows lifted this time. "Are you so sure?" He folded his arms across his chest.

"Haven't a single doubt. For, sir, while I

15

know you enjoy nothing so much as a challenge with such long odds, think about what your winning would mean. Were I to marry, my shares of respectability would no doubt increase, but my days of freedom would be at an end. I ask you, who else could match your stamina in carousing, gaming, or raising a glass to Bacchus?"

"Carousing, eh?" Apsley scratched his temple in feigned contemplation. "I thought you had vowed to become respectable after your failure with Lady Henceforth."

"Allow me to rephrase. Carousing in more intimate circles. In society, I will remain the mannered gentleman and redeem myself for the sake of the MacLaren name."

"So that is what you were doing just now in the garden with the baroness—redeeming yourself?" Apsley raised his eyebrows. "She's married you know."

"Yes, but I've heard he's a poor shot." Laird grinned at his own coarse joke. He'd had an unfortunate start in London this time, that's all. Tomorrow he would do better. And in time he would finally prove himself worthy of his title and of the good widow Lady Henceforth.

He smoothed down his lapels, straightened his back, and fashioned a confident smile.

The click of heels on the marble floor drew the curtain on any further comment on the subject.

"Here comes your mother again."

Laird sighed resignedly. "I apologize, Apsley. I fear there is no escape for you."

Apsley fashioned a shudder as Laird's damning words reached his ears, but hoisted a smile onto his lips and turned in the direction of the drawing room. "Lady MacLaren, how are you this evening?" He glanced momentarily back at Laird. "You owe me one, you do realize this?" he whispered.

"I do, and I truly appreciate your sacrifice." Then, with a chuckle, he nudged Apsley mercilessly forward and into the countess's clutches.

Laird drew in a deep breath and fired it through his teeth as he leaned against the wall nearest the door. The drawing room was more populated with guests than it had been only an hour before.

Ladies garbed in flowing silken gowns stood uncomfortably elbow-to-elbow with dark-coated gentlemen. Naught but narrow rivulets of unoccupied space ran between the clusters of conversation, and those existed only to allow the footmen to continue their libation service.

He peered through the open door at the clock in the passage and huffed a sigh. Damn it all, not yet half-past eleven; it was early by society's standards. Still, he would have left the infernal rout long ago were it not being held in his own bloody town house.

He should not have allowed his mother, who was just fully out from mourning both his father and his brother, to arrange such a grand event here in Cockspur Street.

Clearly he had gone mad.

Why had he not convinced her to wait until autumn, then toss a country house party at Mac-Laren Hall? But he knew this was an idle wish, for she was the Countess MacLaren, and had earned a reputation for doing nothing by half.

Her rout, marking the MacLaren return to society, had been the talk of the *ton* for more than eight weeks. Why, the London newspapers had dedicated nearly as much column space to the impending fête as they had to the goings-on at Parliament. Sadly, it seemed that he alone had dreaded this much-touted event.

Laird thumped the back of his head against a

wall in frustration. He had naught in common with these society boors. Nothing at all.

He wanted to be at Covent Garden or backstage at the opera with all the pretty dancers. Not here, hobnobbing it up with the Quality's white skirts and their starched elders.

But he was the new earl, and he owed it to his family to uphold the honor of the title.

He knew, too, that it was his mother's greatest hope that this night her only surviving son would meet a woman and escort her down the aisle of St. George's by season's end. And so, for her sake, he tried to be charming, to push aside his sadness.

Still, the only women who interested him in the least were two who eagerly offered to join him in the garden and tamp down his pain as effectively as a glass of fine brandy.

But nothing ever lasted long enough this night. Not the spirits, not the carnal pleasures. His emptiness, feelings of loss, of guilt, soon returned redoubled.

With a sigh, Laird scanned the room for a pretty someone to elevate his disposition during this endless affair, when his gaze lit on a tray-bearing footman who was busily dispensing claret to the guests.

Ah, there was his salvation.

He was about to push off from his propped position against the wall when suddenly a pale female seemed to emerge from the plaster not a shoulder's width from him. An odd shiver seemed to tease every bit of his skin at once.

She was a startling vision, swathed completely in white, and he could not manage to remove his gaze from her as she drifted into the center of the drawing room, seemingly unseen by anyone other than himself.

Gorblimey. Could it be that he was imagining this?

He shook his head, wanting to be sure she was actually there, then widened his eyes and focused his gaze entirely on her.

The woman's hair was as pale as sunlight on a winter's morn, and her skin as snowy and smooth as fine porcelain—an angel incarnate.

Or at least this was his first impression of her, though Laird was willing enough to mark this one down to having indulged himself too generously. Admittedly he was defeated by the heavy, numbing effect of the spirits on both his mind and body.

He should have turned for his bedchamber at

that moment, but instead, he took a wobbly step toward her, then another.

And then he witnessed a most astonishing sight.

The angel walked up to a trio of gentleman in the midst of a lively discussion, and without one of them noticing her or what she was doing, she eased a glass of claret from the shortest man's hand, then turned and settled it upon a passing footman's tray.

Damned odd thing for her—or anyone—to do.

And yet, to his astonishment, she repeated the sequence again. This time she lifted a glass from a giggling debutante, too absorbed in her own conversation to notice the crystal's removal from her hand.

What the hell was she about? Didn't make a damned bit of sense.

Just then a footman passed by Laird, pausing only long enough to allow him to lift a filled goblet from the silver salver.

A diverting thought swept into his mind, setting a mischievous grin on his mouth.

Hurriedly he followed the angel as she slowly moved through the crowded drawing room. He watched intently as she looked this way and that for her next victim.

Good, good, she was coming his way now. He would play her game. *Just a little closer. That's right.*

He slipped into the fringe of a lively conversation, and then hoping his apparent inattention would mark him as her prey, began to laugh uproariously as though some great joke had just been told.

He knew the exact moment her attention fixed on him. A thrill shot through his body as she neared, and he felt the pull of warm air as she circled the group, calculating her moment.

His heart pounded hard inside his chest, but he didn't dare look up. Instead he watched her from the periphery of his vision.

Closer and closer she came.

Then it happened.

Her slender gloved fingers pinched the thin lip of his goblet and began to lift.

His free hand shot through the air between them, and before she could register what was happening, he seized her wrist and held firm.

She gasped in surprise and swung her head around and up to look at him.

Laird's breath left his lungs in a whoosh the moment their gazes locked. His left eyebrow shot toward his hairline.

Damn me.

Though her hair, skin, and even her gown were nearly colorless, her lips and her cheeks were the same hue as cherry blossoms in the spring.

But it was her eyes that held him fast. Twin bursts of radiant gold, rimmed with the green of summer, blazed up at him.

Neither he nor she moved or said a word for a minute, or perhaps for a blink. He didn't quite know. Time seemed to cease to exist in that small space they occupied.

Until, all of a sudden, she slyly arched a single golden eyebrow, almost as though she were mimicking him. In a quick movement, she twisted her wrist from him, then turned and ducked into a gaggle of strolling matrons.

In that instant, she was gone.

The corners of Laird's parched lips lifted as he stared into the direction she had disappeared.

Absently he raised his hand to sip from his goblet. But he realized too late that it wasn't there.

The golden-eyed minx had managed to take it after all.

He laughed into his fist, until he realized his grave error.

Bloody hell. She had a fire within her, that one. Might even have been the only woman tonight in whom he held any interest . . . and he hadn't even thought to ask her name.

It was nearly two in the morn, and yet the rout showed no sign of drawing to a close.

But it really didn't matter, Anne decided. Within an hour, she would be home in bed . . . or in shackles. Her temples throbbed madly at the thought.

"Anne, Lilywhite has given the signal." Elizabeth turned from her sentrylike position beside the cold hearth and looked straight at Anne. "The passage is completely clear. *Go.* Go now."

Threadlike wisps of hair rose up at the back of her slender neck. "This is insanity, Elizabeth. I cannot do it, I simply cannot."

"Yes, you can. You know you must. There's no other way. This is our only chance."

"But there are still at least three score guests in the house. What if I am seen? What if I am caught—again?"

"Oh Anne, stop fretting. That gentleman was of no consequence whatsoever. Lud, you were

24

playing a game, and who among us hasn't ever done so at a rout?"

"It was *not* a game, Elizabeth. I was flexing my skills, gathering my courage. But then he *saw me* when no one did. Don't you understand? I am not ready to do this. *He saw me.*" Anne glanced worriedly down the passage in the direction of the staircase.

"What does it matter if he noticed you? He was completely sotted. It is not as though he will remember you." Elizabeth snatched up Anne's wrist. "Besides, the Old Rakes are at the ready in the event anything goes awry. Look yonder." She tipped her head to an elderly, apple-shaped gentleman standing just inside the drawing room doors scratching his ample belly. "Do you see? Lilywhite is just there."

"Is the earl in the drawing room?" Anne swept the room with her gaze. "Because if he isn't, he might have retired to his bed for the evening. Has anyone considered that?"

"How, pray, would I know? He has not been in society for more than a year, so I cannot identify him, either. But Lilywhite has been positioned at the stairs for almost an hour. No one has passed him."

"I cannot go, Elizabeth." Anne's entire body began to quake.

"Yes, you can." She nudged Anne forward a step. "No one else can do this, sister. You know that."

Anne stared mutely at Elizabeth.

She *did* know it.

Their sister, Mary, plump and in her sixth month of pregnancy, was off happily rusticating in the country with her adoring husband.

And as insane as this idea was, Anne knew copper-haired Elizabeth couldn't take three steps through this crowd without earning the admiration of a gentleman or two.

Such was not the reality for Anne. Until this very moment, it had always pricked at her that no one ever assigned her any consequence or bothered to know her name.

But why should anyone pay her heed? She was simply Anne, the middle Royle sister. The one who minded her manners. The one who followed the rules and never purposely did anything that might bring undue notice to herself or her family.

Well . . . at least until tonight.

Anne cast a nervous glance through the open

drawing room doors at Lilywhite. He flashed his eyes at her and raised his chin, indicating her path.

"*Go*, Anne."

She nodded and, with a nervous gulp, started forward.

Until now, more than anything, she had wanted to be noticed, to be seen. To be appreciated.

But on this particular evening, as she snaked her way through an elegant drawing room filled with the frothy cream of London society, Anne purposely did not raise her golden eyes or make any attempt to prompt an introduction to anyone.

She had to rely on her talent for remaining unnoticed. Invisible.

For her very future depended on it.

Lifting the hem of her gown from the floor, she made her way toward the grand staircase leading up to the earl's bedchamber.

Her heart thudded against her ribs as she crept up the treads to the second floor.

She set her ear to the door and listened. Only silence greeted her. And so she felt for the escutcheon, then bent and peered through the narrow keyhole. There was no candlelight within. No light at all. Only darkness.

She straightened and stood. Lud, her corset suddenly seemed abnormally tight. The simple act of filling her lungs became difficult, and her breaths ever thin.

This is madness. Madness!

Why, she could scarce catch her breath. But in her heart she knew there was no turning back.

Carefully she set the tips of her fingers on the latch, pressed down, then slipped inside the darkened chamber, easing the door closed behind her.

Heavens, she was actually here—*in the earl's chamber.*

Everything depended on her now. She had to find the letters. She must.

The Old Rakes had said this was their one and only chance. Wait any longer, and the new earl might find them first and deliver them to the Prince Regent. She had to risk it.

Anne blinked her eyes and waited for them to adjust, but not a sliver of moonlight penetrated the bedchamber. The darkness was as completely black as a swath of thick velvet.

If she could just locate the window and part

the curtains to the pale moon. Even as it was rising earlier, the full moon had seemed abnormally close. Its light blue glow might provide enough illumination to assist her in her search.

Her heartbeat pulsed within her ears as she raised her hands before her, and with fingers spread wide, blindly felt her way around the perimeter of the bedchamber until she found the windows.

She grasped the center part in the smooth satin fabric, and at once whisked back the curtains, allowing a flood of cool light to wash into the room.

At once there was rustling behind her, and she whirled around to see a huge shadow moving in her direction. Her eyes went wide with fear.

Lord help her.

She was not alone.

Chapter 2

How to Become Betrothed
in Two Minutes or Less

My God, could it be?
Laird slid from the massive, oak tester bed and blinked his bleary eyes, quite unable to believe what he was seeing.

But there she was.

His ethereal angel, here, standing in the moonlight in his father's bedchamber.

No. Laird pinched the damp inner corners of his eyes with his thumb and index finger. No, no longer his father's bedchamber, his . . . the town house on Cockspur was his now.

She spun around, turning from the brightness of the window to stare into darkness. Her form became a dark silhouette framed by quicksilver.

He couldn't see her delicate face or her amazing golden eyes.

"Who is there?" Her voice was weak, her stance tremulous. She leaned forward out of the well-lit window bay behind her so that her gaze might better pierce the darkness.

She couldn't see him, he knew, but she was aware he was there.

After all, she had come to him.

Why, he didn't know. Didn't damned well care.

His mind floundered in the swirl of brandy his emptiness had bid him to consume. Walking was near beyond him, and he barely managed to remain on his feet as he slowly made his way toward her.

She sensed his presence drawing closer, and nervously slid a foot backward as if to escape him. "Please, who is there?"

There was loud creak as her heel slammed into the skirting-board beneath the window. A thump as her back met a pane of rippled glass. She could retreat no farther.

"It is just me, my angel," he told her. "No need to run."

Laird came into the light and stood directly before her.

She did not look up at him at first, but peered furtively down at her slippers. Her chest rose and fell rapidly, and he knew she was uneasy. Her quick, shallow breaths fell softly against the wedge of his bared chest, where his shirt had come open as he had unsuccessfully attempted to sleep off the potent effects of the spirits.

"Do not worry," he said to her. He smoothed a hand down the length of her arm.

A small gasp broke through her lips, and finally she lifted her chin. As she turned her eyes to peer up at him, a whisper of moonlight caressed her face. "I . . . I . . . I can't—"

Laird eased his fingers over her cheek, then cupped her chin in his hand and angled her mouth upward toward his. "Yes, you can. You possessed the boldness to come into my bedchamber."

"*No.* You don't understand. I can't—" she protested thinly.

He covered her mouth with his own then, and muted any feeble protest. Her lips were soft and warm, and after a moment he felt them moving against his.

He groaned and slipped his right arm around

her slim waist, and drew her closer so that he could feel her body against him.

She responded with a firm hand against his bared chest, pushing against him at first, but then he felt her fingers ride up his skin and catch the half-tied neck cloth she found there. Her grip tightened around it, and she pulled hard.

It took him a half tick of the minute hand to realize she was trying to hold herself upright.

Confused, Laird drew back a hand's width. Her frightened eyes met his gaze for a scant moment before her knees buckled beneath her.

Her free hand scrabbled at the stays beneath her bodice. "I-I can't *breathe*," she managed, before her grip upon his neck cloth loosened, her eyes closing as she collapsed in his arms.

Anne squeezed her eyes shut and kept them that way, though every instinct begged her to open them.

This cannot be happening.

But it was.

Anne was aware she was being moved onto something soft . . . a carpet . . . no, no, a bed. Yes.

His bed.

But now there was something more.

Do not open your eyes. Just think. Think!

Oh God. What was he doing?

And then she knew. Large, warm hands were skimming familiarly over her breasts. The ribbon closure of her gown was being tugged, loosened. The fabric parted.

Her stomach began to clench. In another moment all the wine she'd enjoyed earlier, and very expensive wine it must have been, too, would make a return engagement.

She had to break away from him, get out of this bedchamber. But how in heaven and earth could she do it? Elizabeth and Lilywhite had no idea she was in need of rescue. And at the moment, the only advantage she had over the man pawing at her person was the fact that he still thought her incapacitated.

Strong, muscled arms turned her and flipped her roughly onto her belly, and fingers fumbled at the ties of her corset—*opening it.*

No, he wasn't—

Anne's eyes snapped wide open, just as she was rolled onto her back. And she saw *him*.

Dear Lord. It was the man who had caught her plucking crystals of cordial from the guests in the drawing room. The very large, long-legged gentleman.

"Lud, it's *you!*" she gasped. "The gentleman—"

Only now his legs straddled her hips, and he was most certainly not being a gentleman. He was pulling at her gown. He was leaning over her. His mouth was just above hers.

He was going to—

No, no!

Laird bent and moved his face over her lips, hoping to feel a puff of sweet breath.

Please, please breathe, lass.

He set his thumb on her chin and pressed, parting her lips wider. *Breathe.*

Suddenly her eyes snapped open and a shrill scream all but pierced his ears, making them vibrate and throb.

"Bloody hell!" Clapping his palms over them, Laird lurched backward and retreated, scrambling to the head of the tester bed. "Stop your screeching, wench! You fainted—I was only trying to help you to fill your lungs!"

Her lips clamped shut, thankfully ending her infernal shrieking. She crawled up on her knees and began furiously setting her gown to rights.

"You were trying to help—by tearing my clothing from me?" Her eyes were blazing with fury. "A gentleman does not take advantage of an unconscious woman. I mightn't have been in London overlong, but I do recognize a beast when I am in the presence of one."

"No, lass, you have it all wrong. You weren't *breathing*."

Her hands were shaking. "T-turn away, I beg you, whilst I dress," she sputtered as she turned her finger in a tight circle before his nose. "Or at least do show me a modicum of consideration by closing your eyes, and allowing me to preserve what little dignity you have yet to strip away."

Devil take me. He closed his eyes.

It was so easy for her to believe the worst of him. So effortless for everyone to believe ill of him.

But, truth to tell, in the past they were usually justified in doing so.

Not this time.

This time he was being . . . well, chivalrous. He puffed his chest out. *Heroic.*

"Look here, miss, I loosened your corset so you could breathe, 'tis all." He rubbed his throbbing temples with his index fingers. "Are you finished dressing now?"

"Nearly."

There was a shifting of sheets as she scooted from the edge of the tester bed and a light double thump as her slippers hit the floor.

Laird blinked open his eyes. In the moonlight, he could see her arms twisting like a contortionist's as she struggled to reach the corset ribbon dangling down the center of her back.

"Would you like some help, lass?"

She turned her accusing eyes to him. There it was. That glare again.

Christ Almighty, he was genuinely only wishing to assist, after frightening her so, but even in the muted light he could see she clearly thought otherwise. "I will not harm you, nor touch you otherwise. I swear it." He reached out for her.

Her eyes widened instantly. "Stay away from me." She turned and made a sudden dash for the door.

"Oh, dear one, I would not open that door, were I you," he warned.

She stopped and looked back at him, chin tipped impertinently upward. "Why not?"

"You cannot return to the gathering in your

state of undress. All of London society is below. You risk complete ruin the moment you leave this chamber."

She looked back at the door, and her hand hovered over the brass door latch for several seconds. Then she spun around and narrowed her eyes, as if studying him for the truthfulness of his statement.

"I mightn't have the best of reputations amongst the ladies, but you can trust my word. Some might say I am quite an expert when it comes to the subject of ruin."

Her eyes shifted this way and that for several seconds. Then, having obviously come to some sort of decision, she eased one slippered foot forward, then the other.

"Come now. No need to fear me." He swung his long legs over the edge of the bed and beckoned to her.

Her chin remained angled to the ceiling as she walked warily toward the bed, then she whirled around so that her back faced him. "Very well. I fear I am forced to accept your assistance."

Laird chuckled to himself as he began to tighten her corset strings.

"Well now, fancy that," she gibed. "Your fingers are nearly as nimble as a maid's. Clearly you have had some practice in lacing corsets." She looked over her shoulder at him, flicked an eyebrow, and then looked away again.

"You might say that."

"I did."

Laird grinned. She was clearly fraught with nerves, and yet she felt some need to spar with him.

He reached the centermost lacing just then and pulled it tight, holding it so with his fingers. "What were you doing here in my bedchamber? You already stole my goblet. Were you hoping for something more, perhaps?"

She gasped, then looked over her shoulder at him. He stared solemnly back at her. Immediately she tried to dart forward, but Laird closed his fist around the ribbon lacing he held and yanked back at the lacing, leaving her teetering on her heels for a moment, before she lost her balance and collapsed against him.

He ringed her slim waist with his hands to help her stand, when suddenly the door slammed open and the bedchamber was illuminated with bright light.

"Oh . . . my . . . word." The Countess Mac-

Laren stood just inside the bedchamber, with two footmen, each armed with a flickering six-armed candelabra. To her left stood Apsley, and indeed several other gentlemen and ladies he had not had the pleasure of meeting.

"Mother."

"Laird . . . what are you . . . oh dear God in heaven. Such shame, such shame. You promised me you had put this foolishness aside for the good of the family." His mother swallowed hard, then steeled herself and narrowed her gaze. "Laird, who, I must ask, is this young woman sitting upon your lap? Do you even know her name?"

Apsley stepped forward. A mischievous grin curved his lips for but a moment before he spoke. "Well, go on, man. Introduce her to your mother."

Laird lifted the miss from his lap and stood her on her feet, then rose and positioned himself beside her.

The young woman glanced up at him. Her golden eyebrows were drawn, and confusion swirled in her eyes. And damned if he could not have sworn that he saw the flustered miss mouth, *MacLaren?*

"I-I . . ." Laird sputtered. He turned from her and gazed at the countess.

Apsley expelled a dramatic sigh. "Oh, I know it is not how you wished for them to meet, MacLaren, but it has happened. So, please, do allow me." He crossed the room, and after casting a covert wink at Laird, took the young woman's hand and, with a gentle tug to set her body into motion, led her directly before the countess.

"Apsley—" Laird began, but it was too late.

"Allow me to introduce you to"—he took a deep breath, then smiled broadly back at Laird—"your son's *betrothed*."

Chapter 3

How a Lie Becomes the Truth

Damn you, Apsley! Laird's head began to spin like a wagered guinea on the table.

Color trickled from the countess's face, along with all trace of readable expression. "I b-beg your pardon, Apsley. Did you say my son's betrothed? *Laird's?*"

"I did." Apsley's mouth spread into a satisfied grin as he gestured to Laird with the very nose that the earl fully intended to smash. "Tell her. Go on," he prodded.

His mother shook her head slowly, as if she hadn't quite decided on the truth of Apsley's inane claim. "No, no, no. This is utter folly. I am sure of it," she finally said, though not quite convincingly enough.

The countess lifted her quizzing glass and

studied the pale young woman standing before her. She held her words for several breaths before speaking again. "I must say, this is rather difficult to believe. Especially after—" Mindful of the crowd inside the room and hovering in the passage beyond, however, she stifled her remark—a tiny blessing for which Laird was truly grateful.

"This cannot be true." The lack of sureness in her statement was undeniable now. The countess shifted her gaze to rest upon Laird. The edges of her lips twitched mischievously. "But son, you have changed so much this past year . . . can this be true? Can it? I know you have always been one for games, but please, Laird, I must know."

He couldn't meet his mother's gaze. *Damn it all.* Not while the miss was looking over her shoulder at him, her golden eyes pleading with him for help.

Sod it. Just what was he to do now? Lie to his mother? Laugh at Apsley's poorly dealt joke and ruin the miss forever in the process?

Hell, his mind was as blank as the Monday morning gambling slate at White's.

Laird blinked and opened his mouth, but then snapped it shut again. His mind was too muddled with drink. The words would not come. There was no right answer.

"Well, then, what say *you*, miss?" The formidable countess released Laird from her assessing gaze and turned to the trembling young woman. She stepped threateningly closer to her.

Somehow, though, the miss kept her footing firm. And though it was hard to know, given Laird's less-than-choice vantage behind her, judging from the surprised expression on his mother's face, the miss must have raised her startling gold eyes and pierced the older woman's gaze.

The countess dropped her quizzing glass, sending it sliding down its chain to dangle at her bosom. Her patience was at an end. "Well, gel? Have you a tongue?"

Laird hurried forward toward the young woman.

She did not reply immediately, but as Laird neared, he saw that her gaze frantically searched the crowd at the door before fixing upon a portly gentleman. A silent stream of words seemed to pass between them. Then the man nodded to her from amid the rapidly growing crowd of onlookers, and she nodded ever so slightly in response.

And then it happened.

The lass honored his mother by dropping a deep curtsy. When she rose again, a transformation had occurred, for her tone was level and sure. Gone was the quivering, fearful miss of only a moment ago, and in her place stood a strong, confident young woman.

"I assure you, I am quite capable of speaking, Lady MacLaren." She smiled brightly. "I am Miss Anne Royle, late of Cornwall, now residing in Berkeley Square with my great-aunt and sister."

Laird did not miss the quick glance Miss Royle gave him, as if making sure he had heard her name.

"Are you my son's intended, Miss Royle?" the countess demanded to know. "Answer me, child. Now is not the time for folly."

"Yes, Lady MacLaren." She squared her shoulders then, and straightened her back. "*I am his betrothed*. He asked me for a moment alone, and we came in here for but an instant—and then he asked for my hand. How fortuitous for us both that you, Lady MacLaren, have arrived to share our joyous moment."

"Oh yes, quite fortuitous," Apsley chimed in

as he waggled his eyebrows mockingly at Laird.

"Joyous, are you, gel?" The countess lifted her chin and peered up into Miss Royle's face. "Then why did you scream?"

Miss Royle angled her head downward and looked at the much shorter countess, and then she raised her head and surveyed her audience. She laughed softly. "Oh my. I daresay, is that what drove the party up the staircase?"

"Yes, Miss Royle," Apsley said, "though it took a few minutes to ascertain from which chamber the cry had originated." He brought a foot forward and leaned close. "Why *did* you scream?"

"Why, from excitement, of course." She turned, spread her arms wide, and addressed the crowd beyond. "The Earl of MacLaren is going to marry *me*—Anne Royle—a simple miss from Cornwall. Is there any lady amongst your numbers who would not have cried out with . . . um . . . *exhilaration*?"

Mamas looked questioningly at their daughters, husbands at their wives. And as if cued, they all shook their heads.

"And you, Lady MacLaren. Certainly you of all gentle people would understand what a great honor your son has bestowed by offering for me."

Within a breath, his mother's countenance transmogrified from pinched and angry to accepting, and finally to beaming brightly with happiness.

Blast! Laird could not believe what he was witnessing. Was Miss Royle in league with Apsley in some grand scheme to win their wager? No, this mad string of events was beyond even Apsley's ability.

Damn it all.

This is not happening.

Ominous black specks ringed Laird's head like a murder of ravens.

He had been wrong earlier. The night could have gotten worse. Much, much worse.

And by God, it had.

The next hour was a complete blur to Anne. Though that was certainly for the best.

Had she any time to contemplate the consequences of claiming to be the Earl of MacLaren's betrothed—an act worthy of plopping her straight into Bedlam—she might have instead flung open the sash and leapt slippers-first from the bedchamber window.

Yes, had she thought about it, *really* thought

about it, she would have infinitely preferred risking a few snapped bones to subjecting herself to the paste smiles and leering judgmental looks the *ton* would eventually bequeath her—when they learned the truth of her lie.

But she had had no choice. None at all.

Thank heavens she had an ally. For the moment, anyway.

Not the earl, her rakish, inebriated, unwitting partner in this night's horribly botched crime.

No, her ardent supporter, as unlikely as it was, was none other than the esteemed Lady MacLaren herself.

For it had been only an instant after Anne uttered her great untruth that the countess had whirled about and faced the gathering. "Please, please," she had called out, reducing the excited chatter in the room to a few whispers. "Let us all retire to the drawing room—to celebrate!" she sang out happily.

A mite too happily.

The countess's hawkish gaze flitted upon each individual in the crowd, almost as though she were taking mental note of the lucky few who had managed to make their way inside the bedchamber to witness the spectacularly scandalous goings-on.

"Come, now, I believe a toast is in order," she twittered as she excitedly waved her gloved hands, shooing the hovering group back into the short passage. There they merged with a growing wave of curious members of the *ton*, and then, after an impervious nod from the countess, were swept back down the staircase by an army of stern liveried footmen.

Anne, realizing her opportunity for escape lay in this moment, had made for the staircase and attempted to plunge into the ebbing tide of confused guests. But her effort was futile. Lady MacLaren had nabbed her in an instant.

"Not *you*, my dear Miss Royle." The Lady MacLaren's surprisingly strong hand gripped Anne's upper arm. "You must come with me to my bedchamber. We have much to discuss."

Before Anne had realized what was happening, she was sitting before a petite dressing table, and the countess's own French lady's maid was busily coiling and repinning her hair, lightly powdering her face, and rouging her cheeks.

"I do not how this engagement truly came about, Miss Royle, but it doesn't matter to me in the least anymore. In fact, the less I know about the horrid details, so much the better." Lady MacLaren snapped her fingers at her lady's maid. "Pull her hair up tighter, and smooth down that waviness. I need her to appear elegant and polished. Do you understand?"

"*Oui*, madame," the maid muttered.

"You and my son were caught alone in the darkness of his bedchamber. I do not know why you were there or for how long, but that is of no consequence. This delicate situation must be addressed carefully and quickly if we are to stop tongues from wagging and soiling your name—and ours."

Anne had no clue what the countess was meaning to do, but at least the woman was aware that there was no true engagement. "Oh, I am so glad you understand. I was concerned you were not aware that this talk of our betrothal is naught but—"

"Miss Royle"—the countess raised her hand and stopped Anne's words—"it matters not. Do not force me to repeat my words. Our course is set now, for I vow, I will not be disgraced again. Not *again*, do you understand me, Miss Royle?"

Anne furrowed her brow. "A-actually no, I don't understand, Lady MacLaren."

But the countess paid her comment no heed. Instead she turned her droopily lidded eyes upon Anne. "Your bone structure shows breeding, and your height—why, one might say you have almost a regal bearing."

"Th-thank you, Lady MacLaren." Anne resisted the urge to slump her shoulders in defeat and sat up straight and tall upon the tufted stool.

Suddenly the countess jerked Anne to her feet. "Stand up, gel, so Solange can see to your lacings.

"Yes, you are quite a lovely woman. That is something at least." The countess sighed loudly. "I must admit, from the first I saw you, dear, your countenance reminded me somewhat of my own in younger years. You are quite fetching. I can see why my Laird would show you favor." The mounts of the countess's plump cheeks rose up as she grimaced, pressing her eyes to thin slits. "Oh, he knows just how to vex me. Always has."

Anne stared at the countess as the shorter woman began to pace the bedchamber. It did not seem to Anne that the countess was addressing her, so much as she was indulging herself in a bombastic rant.

The older woman's hand chopped the air as if she were lopping off heads. "If only he would have considered a proper engagement this time. But there is no help for it now, is there? It is done and we must all live with the consequences. The fact remains that society expects a wedding, and a wedding we shall have."

"A wedding?" Surely the countess could not expect her and the earl to marry just so that the grand Lady MacLaren could avoid embarrassment! He was a rake, a cad of the worst sort. His reputation was as black as boot polish! "You are not serious, Lady MacLaren. I cannot—"

Solange pressed Anne's shoulder and sat her down on the stool once more. *"Parfum,"* the lady's maid whispered as she opened a vial of scent.

"I am always serious, Miss Royle, and the sooner you realize that this is no trifling matter, so much the better." The countess came to stand behind her and spoke to Anne's reflection in the mirror. "It's high time Laird took a wife and assumed his position in this family seriously. Told him so, thrice this very day. So, although yours was not the proper, well-planned betrothal announcement I had hoped for my son, a quick wedding is the best solution for us all."

"I cannot do this. I will not have my reputation sullied by a connection with him!" Anne turned, gingerly caught the countess's hand, and peered up into the older woman's surprised eyes. She held her gaze firmly. "I *will* not."

Lady MacLaren stared down at Anne and gave a haughty laugh. "My dear, you have no choice in this. This is the only way to save your status. If you do not marry my son, your reputation will be irreparably damaged."

Heat sprang into Anne's eyes. "You do not understand. I will not marry the earl. I have heard of him, of course, but I do not even know him."

"No, Miss Royle. It is quite evident to me that *you* do not understand. You—*and* the sister you mentioned to me—will be ruined. Completely ruined. No family will wish a connection with the Royle sisters. Think of her, if you will not consider yourself."

Anne released her grip, pulling her hand away from Lady MacLaren's. She turned around and stared blankly into the hazy vanity mirror.

She would not go through with this. She had not come all the way from Cornwall to prove her noble heritage, only to be connected with the most despicable rake in the realm. She could not. No, there had to be another way.

It was then that she noticed that the countess had become uncharacteristically silent.

Anne looked up. Lud, the older woman was studying her again in the mirror's silver reflection. No part of Anne's body seemed tó escape her scrutiny.

"Good hips," the countess murmured to herself. "Birthing an heir should be no problem."

Bitterly, Anne realized she felt like a calf at a Cornwall livestock market. Heat shot into her cheeks. How dare the countess assess her person in such a way! This was humiliating.

What next? Would Lady MacLaren ask her to open her mouth and show her teeth?

Then Anne saw that Lady MacLaren's expression was not critical at all, which was queer to say the least, given the fact that Anne had been exposed in her son's bedchamber only minutes ago.

Anne leaned closer to the mirror and looked hard at Lady MacLaren's visage. Why, the countess was nodding her head approvingly. La, she almost appeared *appreciative*.

Anne lurched back on the plump stool and turned her body completely around to look at her.

"I daresay," the countess continued. "It seems you are also a woman of very few utterances."

"I am rather reserved, Lady MacLaren, but when I choose to speak I do not mince my words," Anne replied softly.

"That you do. On that point, we agree." The countess was twittering. Indeed, her whole demeanor seemed to change within the span of a breath. "Besides, I cannot fault you for keeping to yourself, my dear. No doubt you are stunned after tonight's surprise . . . er . . . Miss Royle, it *was* a surprise, was it not?"

"Why, y-yes, Lady MacLaren. A *complete* surprise." At least that was not a lie. Until Apsley said she was Lord MacLaren's intended, the idea of a betrothal never entered her mind. And why would it have? The notion had been—and was—insanity!

"Surprise is good. We shall adhere to that part of the story." Lady MacLaren chewed her lower lip. "Of course, I will be asked if your family was aware that your engagement was a possibility, even if I was not. My son has always been an impulsive lad, so if your family is as unprepared for this occurrence as I, we must dispatch Laird at once to receive the blessing of your parents."

"I beg your pardon, Lady MacLaren, but I should inform you that my parents have passed on. My sister Elizabeth and I reside with our great-aunt, Mrs. Prudence Winks, on Berkeley Square." Anne shifted her stance so she might better look Lady MacLaren in the eyes. "But my guardian, Sir Lumley Lilywhite, is well aware of the betrothal. In fact, he is amongst the guests in the drawing room."

"*Sir Lumley Lilywhite?*" What Anne could only identify as an expression of absolute astonishment lit the countess's eyes.

Anne nodded warily. "Y-yes, Lady Mac-Laren."

The countess slapped a gloved palm to her heart. "Good heavens, such a happy coincidence. Dear gel, did he tell you that we are well acquainted? La, it has been so long since we last saw each other. Such a delightful man, and so admirably connected."

Anne's brow furrowed in her confusion. Could

she truly be speaking of Lilywhite—of the Old Rakes of Marylebone? It seemed impossible.

The wisp of a smile touched the countess's lips, and for several moments she seemed adrift in cloud of pleasant memories. By the time she met Anne's gaze again, the brightness had hold of her entirely. "He and Malcolm, my late husband, were school chums and remained close until . . . well, I am not certain why they parted ways, only that they did at one time or another."

Anne wrinkled her nose. "Parted ways?"

"Oh, perhaps their friendship faded with the years, as some relations are bound to do. I honestly do not know. But he stopped calling when I came to Town. I missed seeing him terribly. He is such a jovial fellow, you know. Always made me laugh." A tenseness tightened the countess's features, but in a blink she had rebounded. Gone was her earlier sternness and reserve toward Anne. It was if the countess was suddenly seeing Anne anew.

For it suddenly seemed that Anne's association with Lilywhite bequeathed her with new respect from the countess. Indeed, Lady MacLaren's transformation within the next minutes was nothing less than remarkable.

The formerly stern hostess now addressed her as if they were social equals, and began to chatter happily with nary a breath between her sentences. "My husband resided here, in this very town house on Cockspur Street, when Parliament was in session, you see, while my growing sons and I kept primarily to MacLaren Hall."

Anne masked her confusion and madly racing thoughts with a pleasant smile.

Was it possible that if she gave Lady MacLaren no further reason to doubt her intention to wed her son—understanding now that total ruin was her only other path—the countess would remain bright with benevolence. And, perhaps, just perhaps, she would feel no need to set in motion plans to accelerate their union.

Oh, if only that could be so!

Well, she had to do it. She'd do anything to purchase herself a little more time to extricate from this horrible mess.

"Oh, you must come visit with me there, Miss Royle. St. Albans is not so far. Why, if the weather is fair, the journey might be as little as two or three hours." She laced her fingers. "Yes, you must come and stay for a time. My husband was so proud of his estate, and you will see why. I always thought it a pity that his duties kept him in London for months at a time. He so enjoyed the country. Laird, well, the boy seems to have taken to Town. But now that he is to be married, perhaps that will change."

Lady MacLaren paused, and Anne knew she ought to say something. She ought to set her own shyness aside and become the bold woman she had pretended to be when she stood before society in the bedchamber—telling the most enormous lie of her lifetime. "You are so well known within the ranks of society, Lady MacLaren," she managed, "surely you must have come to London regularly." Not the most enlightened of responses, but passable, Anne decided.

"Alas, not as often I would have chosen. My husband oft reminded me that our family's presence would distract him from his duty to the Crown. So for the good of the kingdom . . ." Lady MacLaren's thought trailed into nothing. "Well, it was the way of things."

Anne shared a sad smile with the countess.

"Besides, it is not the number of days spent in Town that makes a lady memorable." Her spirits visibly lifted. "It is the grandeur of her parties!

Do not fear, Miss Royle from the wilds of Cornwall. I shall instruct you in the art of entertaining well."

Smiling all the while, she straightened Anne's ivory skirt, and then stole a quick glance in the mirror at herself. "Are you ready to face your audience now, Miss Royle?"

Anne stared into the looking glass at the startled visage. Tonight, her worst nightmare had come to life.

I shall never be ready for this. Never.

Still, Anne knew it was impossible to forestall the inevitable, and so she responded by meekly lifting the corners of her mouth.

"Grand. Come with me now, Miss Royle. Our guests await!" With that, she took Anne firmly by the arm, and together they descended the stairs. "I will introduce you to every esteemed guest who had the manners and good sense to remain in the drawing room despite the late hour. Don't you fret at all. Leave the talking to me and all will be well. You'll see."

As they entered the elegant drawing room, the gathering of gentlefolk hushed momentarily before a roar of applause rolled toward them.

Heat surged into Anne's cheeks. Never before

had she been afforded so much attention, and lud, she hadn't even an inkling how to manage it.

Several moments passed before it occurred to Anne that were she truly just betrothed, she would seek out her future husband and join him. She had to make this charade of their betrothal believable this night, did she not?

Anne rose up onto her toes and gazed about the room for her *intended*. Emotions battled inside her as she found herself simultaneously wishing for and fearing his presence.

She hadn't seen the earl since, blank-faced and stunned, he was literally dragged from the bedchamber by well-wishers and his horrid friend Apsley.

All at once clusters of regal ladies cinched around Anne like a very dear satin ribbon, suffocating her with their attentions. Making her, horror of all horrors, the pulsing heart of all activity.

The countess wrapped her arm around Anne's waist. It was as if she was reluctant to let loose the miss who would make her grandest dream for such a wayward son come true. It no longer seemed to matter to the countess that their engagement was naught but a convenient lie.

The engagement was real enough now.

Within minutes, it became all too clear to Anne, if not everyone else, that the countess's intention was to polish the story of her son's shoddy introduction of his betrothed to society until it gleamed like sterling.

It did not seem to disconcert Lady MacLaren that at least a dozen of London's finest had witnessed the event unfolding. Her truth was the one her guests would retell—or risk the cut direct from London's premier hostess.

Anne had never seen such unabashed self-assurance in a woman as she saw in Lady MacLaren. How she wished she could be so confident! But as the minutes passed, and the countess finally left her side to browbeat everyone into agreeing with her version of this night's betrothal tale, Anne began to realize that, oddly enough, she was not quite as unnerved by the assiduous notice as she first had been.

Suddenly her solution became as clear as the crystal goblets she had snatched from bejeweled fingers earlier that evening.

Yes, all she had to do was feign confidence and pretend she really was the woman the earl loved so well as to offer for her.

"Miss Royle?" A deep voice hummed in her ear.

All the courage she had just drawn suddenly trickled from her limbs as she turned and looked up to see the Earl of MacLaren standing beside her.

"*Darling.*" The sarcasm in his tone was as thick and cloying as treacle. "Would you care to join me in the library?"

"The library, my lord?" The sudden dusting of air on her widening eyes stung like sand, sending her lids blinking uncontrollably. "I am sorry, my lord, but I do not believe I *care* to join you just now. I must assist Lady MacLaren in seeing to the guests—"

The earl raised a single brow, the same unnerving way he had when he caught her stealing his goblet earlier. "Allow me to rephrase my request. *Do* join me in the library, Miss Royle. The guests are well-tended."

A large, warm hand pressed against the small of her back and nudged her forward toward the passage.

"Anne!" Just then, Elizabeth managed to reach her side. Her eyes were wild with worry. "Lilywhite desires to speak with you . . . most urgently." She gestured to Lilywhite, who struggled to wedge his generous form between the wall and a ring of cackling matrons surrounding Lady MacLaren.

The earl lifted his possessive palm from her back and folded her arm over his, securing it against his side. "I shan't detain Miss Royle overlong."

Elizabeth scurried around them and tried to block their entry into the passage, but the hulking earl surged forward, causing her to leap from his path. "Please, my lord, won't you wait but a moment longer? He comes this way." When Elizabeth saw that the earl paid her no heed, her concerned eyes turned from the earl's to Anne's own.

Anne reached out, just managing to brush her sister's outstretched hand as they passed her. "No need to fret, sister. I shan't leave without you. Go enjoy yourself, Elizabeth, for this is a celebration." She looked meaningfully at her sister. "I shall join you both very soon," Anne called back over her shoulder as MacLaren pulled her into the passage and trotted her down its length to the dark library.

Two footmen entered behind them. The shorter of the two, with deep pockmarks pitting his round face, hurriedly lit the candles in the sconces on either side of a cold fireplace, while the other, tall and lean, illuminated the candelabra upon the long desk near the window overlooking the garden.

Anne's heart thudded smartly against her rib cage. Slowly she turned around to look at MacLaren. It was just as she'd feared. His countenance was cold and impassive. His gaze, hard.

Then he took a purposeful stride toward her. "You and I have *much* to discuss . . . *my love*."

Chapter 4

How to Excavate Your Own Grave

"**M**y lord, you well know that I did not conjure this ludicrous fantasy that I was your betrothed! It was your ... your—that depraved Apsley fellow," Anne sputtered.

The earl said nothing, which sent her stomach fluttering like a frightened fledgling. "You *know* I had no choice but to follow his lead and claim to be your betrothed. I was facing my ruin!"

"You may yet." He took another step toward her, and lud, if he wasn't beginning to look rather red about the face. "Though Apsley denies it, I must ask if the two of you concocted this scheme together."

"My lord, I assure you I am not, nor have I ever been, in league with your devilish friend." Anne zigzagged her left foot backward, and then leaned her weight upon that leg. The additional half step wasn't much, but at least she was not within his reach if he decided to throttle her, which, were she in his place, she certainly might have considered.

"Will you swear to this?" He cocked his eyebrow again.

Anne set her hands on her hips. "My lord, I am simply a victim of circumstance, a dreadful, unimaginable situation that forced me to act immediately to preserve my reputation."

"And was your *reputation* at the forefront of your mind when you crept into my bedchamber, Miss Royle?" He raked his fingers through his wavy, raven-black hair, and Anne knew at once that he was not as calm as he would lead her to believe.

Her gaze fixed on the vibrant blue of his tired eyes and the stubble just beginning to shadow his strong, firm jaw. Tonight clearly had not been all jollity and conviviality for him. And something in the dour expression on that wickedly handsome face told her that his demeanor had little to do with her lie. As she looked into his pained eyes, her heart began to ache for him.

Fear of his anger suddenly dissolved.

The urge to open her arms and comfort him propelled Anne toward him without warning. Her arms rose up from her sides, and she reached for him before she realized what she was about to do.

Perdition!

Anne halted and snapped her arms to her sides like a soldier. Hurriedly she dropped her gaze to the floor.

What exactly had he asked her? Oh yes.

She gave a small sigh for effect while she rummaged through her mind for a plausible reason why she might have slipped into the earl's chamber. Then her tongue wrapped around just that.

"Well?" He stepped closer. Though he was not yet standing directly before her, he might as well have been. For he was so tall, his shoulders so broad—why, they were twice the span of her own, at least—that his presence seemed to loom over her like a wall of black storm clouds.

"Miss Royle?"

Anne raised her chin and fixed him with her most offended expression. "If you are intent on wrenching from me my purpose for entering your bedchamber, you will have it. Though I had hoped your manners were more refined than to force my confession."

"I apologize for my wretched comportment. But do continue." As if to prod her, he moved again, and now he truly was looming.

Anne swallowed down the second lie she was about to tell this night. But, because the scowl pinching his otherwise passably handsome face made her doubt any appeal to his sense of chivalry would be effective, she added a few more words. "I find the thought of admitting my reason for trespassing highly embarrassing. You must understand, I am naught but a common miss from Cornwall."

"Darling, you are anything but common, but nevertheless, I will have your explanation, since it was the impetus for our upcoming nuptials." His voice was deep and resonant, and at this short distance, it rumbled through her body like rolling thunder.

"'Twas the wine, my lord."

"The wine? Was it not to your liking, Miss Royle of Cornwall?"

Anne knew better than to drop her mask to defend herself. "Oh indeed, sir. It was quite extraordinary, but too much for my constitution to bear. I fear I was in dire need of a . . . of a chamber pot . . . and a bit of privacy."

"And did you find one?"

"Wh-what?" Anne stammered. This was maddening! Why couldn't she seem to focus?

"Why, the chamber pot. It is what you had come in search of, was it not?"

"You are vile." Anne did not have to hold her breath to force the heat into her cheeks.

The earl turned his face to the ceiling and forced a hard laugh before looking down at Anne again. "You honestly expect me to believe this story? This, from a woman who only an hour or so before was prancing about the drawing room stealing goblets from unwary guests."

"Ah, yes. Well, there, too, the wine was at fault." Anne shrugged. My, her story was fitting together nicely, wasn't it? "It simply turned my mind topsy-turvy before my belly. And I am very sorry for the trouble I have caused you. Truly, I am."

The disbelieving mirth that lit the earl's eyes faded away.

Anne sucked her lips into her mouth to conceal a burgeoning smile. He believed her now.

Ha! She could see it. "So, we have had our important conversation, no?"

She gathered up a fistful of her skirts, lifting her hem from the floor. "Now then, my lord, if you will just allow me to pass, I will depart your home and leave you to explain this whole mistake to Lady MacLaren." She started forward, but he caught up her arm and pulled her close against him.

"Oh no, darling." His mouth hovered just above her ear. "You are not dipping your hands into the washbasin and strolling through the door. We are united *together* in this muddle, Miss Royle, and until we come upon an explanation that does not brand the two of us liars of the first order, you *will* remain my betrothed."

Anne shook her head vigorously. "No. No, no, no. I know Lady MacLaren has an expectation, but surely you do not. You are as much a victim in this as I—more so. I know that *together* we can come up with a suitable plan to put this nonsensical betrothal aside."

"Yes, I agree, but until this plan of yours surfaces, you are my fiancée."

"You cannot expect me to pose as your intended after this night."

"I mean exactly that." The earl clasped her gloved hand and raised it upward as if he meant to kiss it. She pulled against him, but he would not free her hand. "You seemed so wholly eager earlier in my bedchamber."

The faint scent of brandy lingered on his warm breath, luring her gaze to his mouth, forcing her to remember the way he grabbed her and kissed her in his bedchamber. The way that kiss stole her breath away!

"B-but, my lord, there is a solution—a very simple one. When I return to the drawing room, I will admit I agreed to marry you in haste. I shall blame it on the wine. And then I will cry off. No harm done. We will both be freed from the shackles of this hoax."

The earl shook his head. "No, lass."

"No?" Anne was incredulous. "Why ever not? It is the perfect solution."

"I beg to differ."

"Why is that? I know you have no true wish to marry me. Even in the short time my sisters and I have resided in London, I have heard tales about your wicked ways."

"Indeed?"

"Yes. When I first arrived in Town, I was told

by more than one matron that every young lady should count herself fortunate that you were away for the year, and not in Mayfair dedicating yourself to rending all the gossamer reputations that you might. I cannot be connected with *you*."

He winced at that, making Anne immediately wish she could snatch back her thorny words.

Lord MacLaren cleared his throat quietly before pinning her with his gaze. "Obviously you have not heard everything about me, Miss Royle. Had you, you would have known that Lady Henceforth and I were betrothed until *she* cried off some fifteen months ago."

Anne stared up at him. "You were to be married? *You?* The new Earl of MacLaren, the veriest rake of the realm?"

"Veriest? Hardly. There are worse. Apsley for one." He straightened his back. "But yes, Miss Royle. Yes, I was to be married. She left me standing in the chapel, comforting my distraught mother and making excuses to my embarrassed father."

"I am sorry for that, my lord." She dropped her gaze for but a moment. "So, just to be perfectly clear on the subject, I gather that—"

He did not allow her to finish. "Crying off this eve is not an option I will discuss with you. What else have you? Anything?"

"Oh. Well, I suppose we could . . ." Anne narrowed her eyes and peered up at him. "Wait one moment, sir, why must I craft a plan? I do not hear you offering any impressive ideas."

"And you shan't. I was too deep in my cups to respond properly when you announced our engagement. Therefore, I will call upon you tomorrow evening when I am confident that the brandy has been sufficiently evaporated from my veins."

"Tomorrow?" Anne gasped.

"Yes. Berkeley Square, was it not? Oh yes, one more thing." Lord MacLaren stuffed two fingers into his watch pocket and fumbled about a bit. From the pocket, he withdrew a cabochon sapphire ring, and without comment or explanation, began to slide it onto Anne's finger.

Anne squealed as the ring met with some resistance at the wrinkle of her kid-gloved knuckle, but he did not relent. It was clear that he meant to have that damnable ring on her finger, even if it meant breaking her digit to achieve his goal. He pushed harder and harder still, even as she struggled against him, until at last it rode down to the base of her ring finger.

He released her hand then and smiled at her. It was a warm, wonderful smile—not half as devilish as she might have expected from him. He should let himself smile more often. She'd tell him that, if she did not despise him so just now.

"A betrothal ring," he explained. "It belonged to my grandmother. The countess expects to see you wearing it when we emerge from the library."

"Lord MacLaren, I will not wear it. This only deepens the lie." Anne sucked in a shallow breath and began to tug and twist at the heirloom ring glistening like a night sky. "Blast! I can't move it past my knuckle."

"Good." He smirked.

Having been a proper lady long enough, Anne opened her mouth to assail him with a stinging retort, when suddenly his mouth covered hers. She gasped as his tongue swept inside, and his lips began to move as if he were devouring her.

For the briefest of moments, she could not breathe. The faint taste of brandy was sweet on his tongue, and it warmed her mouth, for just an instant, before he pulled away.

She was stunned for a moment, dizzy and

confused. Anne stared up at him, her lips still throbbing and sensitive from his searing kiss.

The left edge of his lips pulled up in a cocky grin. "Mmm. Not bad by half." He chuckled, then smacked his moist lips together.

Instantly Anne's senses returned with force. The back of her hand flew to her mouth, but she had forgotten about the ring, and instead of displaying her utter distaste for him by wiping his kiss from her lips, she clinked her front tooth loudly with the sapphire.

Heat swept her cheeks. "Y-you are naught but a wicked man." She narrowed her eyes at him. "And to think I actually pitied you this night."

"Oh, you should feel sorry for me. We are both victims."

"Yes, we are. And while everyone in this house might believe we are engaged, we are not. So . . . so please stop taking liberties."

"The kiss was delicious. You must admit that."

"I will not. And it is not as if you had not already kissed me once this night. This was no new experience for you."

The earl chuckled. "Oh, but darling, it was. I am quite certain this was the first time I kissed my *betrothed*."

Chapter 5

How to Use a Boning Knife

It was nearly daybreak when Sir Lumley Lily-white, grumbling beneath his labored breath, ushered Anne and Elizabeth into their sponsor's grand house at Two Cavendish Square in Marylebone.

Anne was exhausted both in mind and body, but not so fully as Lady Upperton appeared to be. Evidently the old woman had not slept at all, but had instead waited up for Lilywhite's couriered report from the MacLaren rout.

Her pale blue eyes were threaded with crimson as she blinked up from the petite settee where she sat awaiting their arrival.

Beleaguered by a bothersome cold upon her chest, she hadn't condescended to change from her bedclothes, despite the expected presence of a gentleman. Instead, Lady Upperton met her guests in a rumpled brocade dressing gown with an embroidered nightcap crowning her curly white hair. Her tiny slipper-clad feet, dangling several inches from the floor, kicked spasmodically the moment her gaze fell upon the Royle sisters.

"Are you absolutely mad?" Lady Upperton shrieked as Lilywhite brusquely angled Anne and Elizabeth toward the settee. "Anne, you said you were his *betrothed*! Oh dear." She raised a finger in the air, then squeezed her eyes tightly closed and readied a handkerchief below her red nose to stifle a sneeze. "A moment, please."

Anne shot a glance over her shoulder at Lilywhite as Lady Upperton waved her lace-edged linen before her face . . . waiting.

"My, good news does travel quickly in London"—Anne looked at her sister—"doesn't it, Elizabeth?"

"This is hardly good news, Anne," Elizabeth chided. "But, la, he is handsome. Have you ever seen eyes that color? They are like sapphires."

"Please do not mention sapphires to me, Elizabeth." Anne cast a furtive glance at the ring on her finger.

Lady Upperton opened her eyes, the sneeze crisis temporarily averted. "Indeed your betrothal is *not* good news! It is dreadful." Lady Upperton settled her handkerchief in her lap and lifted a dainty blue and white cup from the oversized tea table before her. "Lilywhite, be a dear and let the gentlemen know the gels have arrived."

Lilywhite nodded and walked across the library to the column-framed bookcase beside the cold hearth. Though both Anne and Elizabeth had witnessed what he was about to do several times before, it never failed to impress them. They watched as Lilywhite pressed his plump hand to a carved image of a goddess's face on one of the columns. Her pert nose depressed beneath his hand.

No sooner had this occurred than there was a faint click and whine of hinges, and suddenly the lower portion of the huge bookcase swung wide, revealing a secret passage. The portly man shifted his considerable weight from one leg to the other, waddled into the dark opening, and disappeared from sight.

"Dear Lady Upperton, if you will permit me, I will explain everything to your satisfaction."

Anne closed the space between herself and the small, elderly woman, and slid onto the settee beside her.

"Sweeting," Lady Upperton began, "I know you are a clever, resourceful gel, but I cannot fathom what set of events could have passed that would require you to make such an outlandish claim as being Lord MacLaren's betrothed."

"It is not as if I had any other alternative." Anne lifted Lady Upperton's almost child-sized hand and squeezed it, unintentionally wrinkling the woman's translucent skin as if it were made of tissue. "He caught me in his bedchamber, and then I screamed, and the countess—nay, all of society—caught *us* in what could be construed as a most compromising situation. You must know how any sort of attention vexes me. How difficult it was to stand beneath the judgmental gazes of the *ton*—and to be forced to lie."

"But Anne, claiming to be the earl's betrothed! If it is attention you fear, why, child, you've made it worse—you've magnified the notice you will receive from this night forth."

"I did not choose my lie. The earl's friend, Lord Apsley was his name, offered up a somewhat plausible explanation for the two of us being found together in his bedchamber—that we were *betrothed*. I had no choice, at the moment, but to grasp at any explanation he offered."

There was a distinct click of a cane upon the floor. Anne glanced up to see two tall, elegantly dressed elderly gentlemen enter the library through the secret door connecting Lady Upperton's home with the Old Rakes of Marylebone gentlemen's club next door. Sir Lumley, somewhat slower in gait, brought up the rear of the column, and within a moment the three gentlemen had joined the ladies before the settee.

"Lilywhite, you were a damned fool to allow the gel to make such a claim." Lord Lotharian, the self-proclaimed king of the elderly cadre glanced from Lilywhite to Anne, and then shook his head dolefully.

Anne lifted her palms before Lotharian. "I tell you I had *no choice*."

"Well, she could have done worse—even saddled with his notoriously wicked reputation. There is a limited supply of unattached earls in London, you know." Lord Gallantine, whose auburn wig sat slightly askew on his pate, settled his hand on Lotharian's shoulder. "Still, I agree, with my man here. Why, the earl could have just as easily denied the betrothal and pointed out you, Anne, as naught but a thief in the night."

"Yes, he could have, but he did *not* deny it when Apsley tossed the explanation into the air. Instead, he said nothing. And at that moment I knew, *I knew*, claiming to be his betrothed was my only hope of avoiding ruin—or arrest."

Lotharian chuckled at that. "She has a keen eye for human nature, this one. Shall I teach her how to play piquet?"

"You will do nothing of the sort, Lotharian." Lady Upperton turned her cool gaze from the gentleman and affixed it firmly on Anne. "Did you at least find the letters, child?"

"I did not. The rapscallion of an earl caught me the moment I opened the curtains for light."

"How then did you explain your presence in his bedchamber?" The old woman pursed her lips and lifted a white eyebrow questioningly. "Whatever you said must have been quite believable. After all, you are here and not in chains."

"I did not manage to tell him anything before—" Anne rounded her eyes and gulped down a fortifying breath.

Elizabeth hurried to her sister and knelt before

her. "Before what, sister?" She set a hand gently on Anne's knee. "'Tis all right. You can tell us. No matter what he did . . . well, we are here for you. We will always be here for you."

"Wh-what? Oh, good heavens! No." Anne shoved Elizabeth's hand away. "When he grabbed me, he unwittingly stepped on the edge of the floorboard. *The* floorboard, and it started to pop open!"

Lady Upperton gasped and clapped her pudgy fingers to her lips. "He did not see—"

Anne was already shaking her head. "No. I stepped on the rising board and threw myself against him—pretending to faint."

"Quick thinking. She has a knack for this, just as you said, Lotharian." Lilywhite smiled broadly. "Miss Anne, your father would have been so proud of you."

Elizabeth frowned. "What of the letters? Did you see them? Are they still under the floorboard beneath the window?"

Anne grimaced. "I wish I knew. There was no time to look. No time for anything. For the next thing I knew, all of society was barging into the bedchamber and I was forging the grandest lie of my life."

"Oh, Dove, perhaps matters are not so dire as we believe." Lady Upperton sniffed, likely due to the cold upon her chest, and hugged Anne close. "Why, once we have the letters, you will simply cry off."

Anne wearily broke the embrace. "Lady Upperton, I had thought to do just that. But after speaking with the earl privately this evening— la, it is nearly morning . . . *last* evening—I have learned that my path to any sort of resolution will not be direct. It seems I must endure the focus of the *ton* awhile longer."

Lilywhite groaned softly as he lowered his old bones into a chair near the settee. "MacLaren informed the gel he won't have it. Crying off is not an option, he told her." He huffed. "Said he won't have his mother shamed that way again. I reckon 'tis his own shame he is most concerned about, now that he must assume his father's family responsibilities—and likely in the House of Lords as well."

Lord Lotharian poked a bony finger into the air. "But our gel here is the true victim of this scandal, not he nor his sainted mother. Proof of the gels' heritage was stolen and hidden away by his blackheart of a father. She did nothing wrong by trying to retrieve that proof. It is her birthright, I say."

"No, my lord." Anne came slowly to her feet. "Slipping into his bedchamber to steal a cache of secret letters from the Prince of Wales to Maria Fitzherbert, no matter what they might prove, is a crime. I could have been flung into Newgate! Instead MacLaren, as unbelievable as it might seem, protected my honor."

"He might have done so, but I am certain he did not do it purposely. He was sotted." Elizabeth said matter-of-factly. "I am of the belief he was too foxed to react to what was being said just then. Honor, yours or his own, likely never entered his brandy-soaked mind."

"No matter, whether we like it or not, my name is now connected with the Earl of MacLaren." Anne raised her left hand and held it before Lady Upperton's mottled nose. "This is his grandmother's ring, Lady Upperton. His mother wished that I, his betrothed, would wear it."

The old woman seized Anne's hand and brought the ring closer to her eyes. "Dear gel, you cannot keep this."

"Neither can I seem to remove it—nor the

glove now, for that matter." Anne sighed and reached out with her free hand to give the ring one more tug, before turning her gaze to the Old Rakes. "I should have known when you three bade me steal the letters this night, that one way or another I would be shackled."

"Again, I must offer my counsel once more. Marrying the earl is not such a tragic fate, my dear," Gallantine interjected.

"Marrying the earl is not an option. Our betrothal is folly." Anne exhaled in frustration. "You speak as if he actually wishes to marry me. He doesn't! Nor do I wish to marry him. Please, let us not speak of this again. I just want this ring off my finger. Now."

"Oh, sister, do not be so theatrical." Elizabeth snatched up Anne's hand and tried twisting the ring off herself.

"It will not be removed." Anne jerked her hand back. "You are only making my knuckle swell—"

"It *will* come off," Elizabeth countered. "When we return to Berkeley Square, we will just cut it off with Mrs. Polkshank's boning knife and be done with it."

"My finger?" Anne narrowed her eyes. "Or

the ring, Elizabeth? For I am afraid I cannot allow either to be severed without risking imminent death."

"Neither, you silly goose, *the glove*."

Lilywhite cleared his throat. "However we decide to remedy this betrothal problem, we must do it soon. Lord MacLaren has informed me, as well as Anne, that he intends to call this very eve to set the situation to rights."

"Time is of the essence, it seems." Lotharian clapped his hands loudly, startling everyone to attention. "Lady Upperton, will you take on the task of devising a congenial end to Anne's betrothal to MacLaren?"

Lotharian did not even wait for the old woman's reply before turning to Elizabeth. His eyes twinkled with a mischievous gleam. "Elizabeth, dear, I know your cook is extraordinarily skilled in coaxing information from footmen. Will you please ask Mrs. Polkshank to ascertain whether the MacLaren house staff will be off duty tonight? I have heard that Lady MacLaren is generous to the staff in this way after a grand gathering."

Elizabeth nodded blankly.

"Lord Lotharian, why must you know the

whereabouts of the MacLaren house staff?" Anne could not mask the suspicion in her voice. "You are planning something, aren't you? Why, it is plain in your eyes."

"My eyes?" Lotharian laughed.

"If your scheme involves . . ." Anne narrowed her gaze at the old man as it suddenly occurred to her what he might be thinking. "Oh *no*. I will not enter the earl's bedchamber again. I will not do it."

"Darling gel, no one is asking you to do such a thing." Lotharian reached out his long arm and patted her shoulder. "No need to fret."

Anne's tensed muscles had just begun to relax when she glimpsed Lotharian casting a covert wink to his left, sending a brief, almost imperceptible grin to Gallantine's thin lips.

A shiver raced over Anne's skin.

Oh dear God. What now?

Half-past nine of the clock in the evening

The night air, damp from the earlier rain, could almost be called mild, and Laird felt perfectly comfortable walking in his plum-hued kerseymere dress coat. He was neither too cool nor too warm, and the walk from Cockspur Street to Berkeley Square was rather bracing.

Besides, Apsley deserved to walk after what he'd done.

"Pick up your hooves, you addle-pated fool."

"I am not fully to blame, MacLaren. You bloody well bet me I couldn't do it."

Laird didn't respond.

"And the gel, why was she in your bedchamber anyway? You know, I have a notion she saw your vulnerable state and decided to catch you in the parson's mousetrap."

"Do shut up, Apsley."

"I heard that her guardian is Lilywhite, one of the Old Rakes of Marylebone. They're a wicked lot—think they'll allow me to join once I'm gray?—anyway, wouldn't doubt it if we were to learn he put her up to it. Heard they trapped a duke for the older sister. Why not an earl for the blonde chit?" Apsley was already struggling for breath. "Really, MacLaren, I could have called for my landau or a hackney—rather than walk."

"Enough! Like it or not, you are going to help me untangle this bloody knot you've tied." Laird could not bring himself to look at Apsley. "And stop complaining. We're walking."

"Well, I can see that." Apsley huffed, making a great show of his exertion and displeasure. "Sod it all, had I been meant to walk halfway across Town I would have been born a coalman . . . not heir to an earldom."

"The walk will do your constitution good." Laird kept his gaze straight ahead, even as Apsley drew alongside him.

"I am in fine shape. All the ladies tell me so."

"I am sure they do. Until your coat, waistcoat, and shirt are dropped onto the tester bed, and your *chére amie* glimpses your corset."

"No need to bite." Apsley stopped walking. "And it is not as if most gentlemen do not use a corset to achieve a flat stomach."

Laird lengthened his stride. "Most gentlemen of a *certain* age anyway," he murmured, just loud enough for Apsley to hear.

"I say, MacLaren, not all of us are blessed with the physique of Michelangelo's *David*." Apsley trotted along the pavement behind Laird.

"Good God, I would hardly label *David* as wholly *blessed*."

"Mac, forgive me. I'll make it up to you."

"I know you will. I have a plan."

"You know I will help. Whatever you ask, I will do. I swear it." Apsley stretched out his arm, grasped Laird's coat sleeve, and yanked hard, forcing him to spin around in the opposite direction. "But how do you know she will go along with your scheme?"

"She has a name, Miss Anne Royle."

Apsley scratched his temple. "Why does that name sound so damned familiar?"

"Because she is my bloody betrothed!"

"Oh, right." Apsley picked up his trotting pace to match Laird's lengthening stride. "Now that I have apologized, more or less, will you explain why can't we board your carriage? It is bloody well right there—following us like a great shadow!"

Laird shrugged off Apsley's hand and resumed walking down the pavement. "It is in use."

"Pacing us?" Apsley hurried to catch Laird up.

"Transporting something for me."

"What?" Apsley's face contorted in confusion. "What is in the cab that is so damned all-important that we have to walk all the way to Berkeley Square?"

"A gift." Laird grinned to himself. "For my *betrothed*." He reached out and slapped Apsley on the back. "Pick up your pace, man, only another mile to go."

Berkeley Square

The ladies sat in the parlor awaiting Lord Mac-Laren's arrival.

He hadn't bothered to send a card informing Anne of the hour he might be expected. That might indicate he possessed manners, and of course he had none. And so they waited. Two hours so far. Two mind-numbing hours during which Anne was left to fret and imagine the absolute worst endings to the evening.

As was her habit, Aunt Prudence slept in the chair beside the fire, sucking the remnants of cordial from her withered, wine-stained lips.

Cherie, the petite, silent maid-of-all-work, gently lifted the half-empty crystal of cordial from the ancient woman's palsied hand. She settled it on the old sterling salver that MacTavish, the family's gray-haired butler, extended to her, and then quit the room with him.

"Lotharian should have sent word to us by now." Lady Upperton slipped her hand between the drapes, parting them, and peered out the window to the street.

Anne's elbows were propped upon the mantel, and she glanced up, catching movement in the gilt-framed mirror that hung above it. She turned to see Elizabeth entering the room with Mrs. Polkshank, former tavern maid, now their household cook.

"Are you sure of your facts, Mrs. Polkshank?" Elizabeth was asking.

"Oh yes." The cook nodded, sending both her chins and her pendulous breasts bobbing. "Lady MacLaren gave all the staff the night to themselves—the day, too. And not just the serving staff, all of 'em. From the butler right down to her own fancy frog of a lady's maid."

Lady Upperton pulled her nose back from between the drapes and addressed the cook. "And Lord Lotharian was made aware of this—you're certain?"

"Oh, sure as a wench like me can be. Took the message to him meself."

"You?" Anne had never liked the uncouth cook, and she knew the feeling was more than mutual.

Mrs. Polkshank had always preferred Mary, the frugal eldest of the Royle triplets. Mary had hired her, without references, mind you. And paid her handsomely for her ability to steal society guest lists from randy footmen whose brains obviously resided in their breeches.

Now the bawdy cook expected payment for every secret she obtained on behalf of the Royles—which would not be so worrisome, had the cook's requests for payment not doubled each time she was needed to perform . . . a special service.

Mrs. Polkshank smiled cheekily at Anne. "I did. And he, bein' the fine gentleman he is, invited me to sit and take tea with him in the library. He didn't give a fig that I am naught but a cook. He knows a real woman when he sees one. Why, we chatted, just like I was Quality, for at least an hour."

Lady Upperton brought her hand to her crimson-painted lips, concealing a faint smile, then abruptly returned to her post at the window. "Oh my!" She lurched backward suddenly and spun around on the very high heels of her satin slippers. "I never heard the carriage wheels. Dear heavens, the earl is here, and he's brought Lord Apsley with him!"

The percussion of the brass knocker slamming to its base fired through the house like a pistol shot.

Elizabeth raced across from the parlor, grabbed Anne's arm and flung her onto the settee, then took a seat beside her. "Mrs. Polkshank, the tea."

"No, no. Arrack punch." Lady Upperton's pale blue eyes were wild as she leapt up into the wingback chair opposite Aunt Prudence.

"Wait!" Anne held her voice to a hush. "Brandy. That's what they were drinking last night."

"Yes, Miss Anne. Best idea yet. Men do enjoy their brandy, and I ought to know." Mrs. Polkshank poked her chest proudly with her thumb, and then hurried from the parlor.

Despite the disturbance, Aunt Prudence did not awaken. Her eyelids never even fluttered. Her breathing remained slow and steady, whistling softly each time she exhaled through her long nose.

Within an instant MacTavish appeared in the doorway with the gentlemen callers, but stood silently, looking at Lady Upperton, then Aunt Prudence, and then at the Royle sisters.

It was clear that the dyspeptic, ill-tempered Scotsman her penny-pinching sister Mary had engaged as butler—also without a single reference—was unsure which of the ladies to address first. Then, much to Anne's horror, she saw his lips move, and he seemed to silently say: *Ah, sod it.* "My ladies, the Earl of MacLaren, and the Viscount Apsley."

The women instantly came to their feet, with the exception of their great-aunt, of course, who continued to sleep.

Bloody hell.

Laird brought his glass to his mouth and tipped back the rest of his brandy. He and Apsley had endured the pleasantries for nearly half an hour, and not once had Lady Upperton, Miss Royle's sponsor, left her side.

It was time to put an end to this farce. Everyone in the room knew the truth of their betrothal anyway. It was time to act.

"Miss Royle," he blurted, somewhat louder than he meant. "I would have a word, please."

Lady Upperton inserted herself between him and the gel, but before she could manage a protesting word, he reached over the short older lady to Anne and drew her around to his side. "Please."

Elizabeth started forward, but Anne waved

her off. "'Tis all right. Really." She looked up at Laird with those startling golden eyes, and for several brief seconds he quite literally forgot what he was about to say.

"This way, my lord." She led him into the passage, meaning certainly to take him to another room, but he stopped her there.

"I have a plan," he told her, trying to look confident that this would work and that she had nothing to fret. "One that will benefit us both, I assure you."

Miss Anne smiled, a true smile, then exhaled her great relief. "Oh, thank heavens, you've seen the reason in it."

"Reason in what?"

"Why, my crying off, of course."

"Oh, that. Yes, I agree."

Miss Royle relaxed her delicate shoulders. "I am so relieved. You cannot possibly imagine."

Laird laid a vertical finger across her lips, quieting her. "Only you can't cry off just yet."

She grasped his hand and pulled his finger away. "Oh. Then when? Friday? The *Times* is published on Saturday. I am sure the *on-dit* columnist would love to run the story of our short-lived plan to marry."

"You may cry off at the end of the season. I think that should be sufficient time."

"Season's end?" Twin blossoms of pink bloomed on her suddenly anger-pinched face. "That is an impossibility, my lord. How many seasons do you think I have left before I am considered withered on the vine and too old to marry?"

Laird shrugged, knowing any number he gave, any word he spoke just then, would only make her more agitated.

"Well, I shall tell you, my lord. I haven't one to spare! Not one, if I wish a good match in this lifetime." She reached into the placket opening in her skirt, whisked out the betrothal ring she'd hidden there, and slapped it into his palm.

He snatched up her hand and shoved the ring onto her finger once more. "I do apologize if this impedes your husband-hunting endeavors this season, but I am afraid you really do not have an option, Miss Royle."

"My, you are arrogant. Of course I have a choice. And I will not do it." She turned her chin defiantly up at him.

"Yes, you will." He slipped his hand around her slim waist and hurried her to the front door.

"Come, my dear. I have something to show you just outside. I think it might convince you otherwise."

Though she walked along with him easily enough, she struggled against his firm grip.

Laird flung open the front door and gestured to his gleaming town carriage waiting on the street. "See for yourself, lass." With a flick of his finger, Laird signaled the footman to open the cab door.

"I vow that there is nothing that could possibly entice me to change my mind, especially now, you brute!" she snapped as she turned her head and gazed toward the street.

But the moment the carriage door opened, and the footman's lantern illuminated the interior, Miss Royle stopped thrashing and became utterly still.

The color that had risen into her cheeks drained away, and she became instantly pale.

"Except *that*," she conceded.

Chapter 6

How to Catch Spiders

Anne stared with disbelief at the three Old Rakes sitting across from a burly, truncheon-waving Bow Street Runner in the interior of the earl's town carriage. The elderly trio was dressed entirely in black, and, at the moment they were trussed up like hens about to be roasted over a cooking fire.

The earl released Anne from his grip. "So, we are in agreement, Miss Royle? You will assist me until the end of the season? I don't expect my needs will extend beyond then."

Anne tore her gaze from the Old Rakes and glared up at the earl standing at her side. "I do not know what this could possibly be about, but it is clear that you believe you have me at some disadvantage and that I have no alternative but to follow your dictates."

"You have the right of it." The earl cleared his throat. "Though you do have two choices."

"As many as that, two?" Anne folded her arms over her chest.

"We can stand here while I explain why your and your sister's guardians are on their way to Bow Street for questioning tonight. But detailing the events for you might take some time, and who knows who might happen by." He glanced dramatically from side to side as if searching the square for interlopers.

"What is my second choice?" Anne huffed.

"You may simply agree to pose as my betrothed for the duration of the season, and the Old Rakes will be set free. Choose this option and we shall all go inside to discuss my requirements of you this very moment."

"Oh, good Lord." Anne called out to Bow Street Runner, "Put down that bludgeon of yours and let them go, please!" She glowered at the earl. "Now, may we all go inside the house?"

The earl held his hand to ear. "Excuse me, I haven't heard you say—"

"I agree—*I agree.* I will do whatever you ask." Anne looked around the square to be sure no one of account had witnessed the exchange. "Please, my lord, let us all go inside."

"Absolutely, my darling." The earl grinned, and then waved to the Bow Street Runner sitting inside the carriage. "Cut them loose."

Lord Lotharian rubbed into his chafed skin the salve that the maid, Cherie, had slathered on his rope-raw wrists. "The fault of our capture was Gallantine's entirely. I was hoisting myself from the bedchamber window when Gallantine came swinging past, tangling our ropes like a deuced spider's web!"

"Do you think I did it a-purpose? Lilywhite released my line far too quickly. It was either grab for you or shatter my bones on the terrace below."

Lilywhite's plump face glowed like a beacon. "It was your screaming like a schoolgirl that drew the Runners. So I agree with Lotharian. The fault is yours, Gallantine."

The earl chuckled at that. "Actually, the Runners were already in the garden. I engaged them to watch the house for intruders since the staff had been allowed the evening to themselves."

"Why were the guards there to begin with?" Anne asked.

Lord MacLaren lowered his head and looked down at his hands, clearly not wishing to reply.

Apsley settled his hand on his shoulder. "His father was attacked and killed just over a year ago by burglars-*thugs*. They ransacked the house—and then it happened again just one week ago—just before Laird opened the Cockspur town house for the season. I made the report myself. I was passing by when I saw lights inside. Thought MacLaren had come home earlier than expected, but he hadn't. Everything in the house had been turned topsy-turvy. Bloody mess. There were papers everywhere."

"Wait a moment." Elizabeth looked back to Laird. "The burglars killed your father?" she asked gently.

Laird nodded slowly. "He likely surprised them as they were just beginning, for they didn't take anything of note. Much like, I suspect, the Runners surprised the three of you this night, eh?"

"More brandy, my lord?" MacTavish asked during the momentary lull in the conversation.

Laird allowed the butler to fill his crystal with brandy. "When I returned home, after seeing my mother to the Lady Fustian's musicale, imagine my astonishment when a Runner headed me to my garden just as Lilywhite was lowering himself down from the rooftop, by means of some contraption."

"It was a crate hoist I secured from the West India Docks." Lady Upperton was beaming. "Well, not exactly a crate hoist, but rather my miniature adaptation of one that might allow for greater vertical mobility."

"*For burglary.* Clearly the four of you, for it seems I must now include you in their number as well, Lady Upperton, spent a goodly amount of time planning this burglary. One might think that the prize would be very dear."

Lotharian and other two rakes exchanged convert glances.

Laird rose from his chair, reached into his coat pocket, and withdrew an ivory blade. "And yet this small letter opener, or page cutter, perhaps, is all that was removed from my home—and that, it seems, from beneath a loosened floorboard in my bedchamber."

He realized that the Royle sisters had not seen the blade before. Their eyes were curious, and they jockeyed for a better position to see it.

Slowly Laird turned the blade over in his hand,

again and again, aware that every eye in the parlor was fixed on it. "This leads me to believe the blade has a greater significance than its utility in opening letters or separating book pages."

"Might I—" Lotharian crossed to Laird and reached for the ivory blade.

Laird lifted his brow. "Am I mistaken? I was told that the object was found in your possession, Lord Lotharian. Surely you have seen it."

"Well, of course I have. The blade is mine." Lotharian reached out to take it, but Laird whisked the ivory cutter cleanly from the old man's reach.

"Ah, really?" Laird slid the ivory into his pocket again. "Then, pray, my lord, what was etched into the blade?"

Lotharian raised the back of his bony, reddened hand to his forehead and sighed forlornly. "Alas, I do not recall. I am but an old man. My memory is failing."

Miss Anne stepped between Laird and Lotharian. "Enough of this cat-and-mouse game. I told you I would do whatever you asked. Please, just give him back the blade if it is not yours."

"I never claimed it was mine." He watched her face as he slowly grasped the handle of the blade and withdrew it from his pocket. "But it may be *yours*, Miss Royle."

"Mine?"

Laird took her hand, turned her palm flat, and laid the blade upon it. "Do you see? Oh, there are other letters, and numbers, too, but look just there, near the edge of the handle."

Her golden eyes grew wide. Whirling around, Anne hurried to the mantel and held it before the flickering sconce. "R-O-Y-L-E." Her gaze sought out her sister. "Elizabeth, come and see."

Elizabeth rushed to her sister's side. She took the blade from Anne's hands and turned it over in the candlelight before pivoting back around to face the congregation. "Why, you are correct, Lord MacLaren. This must have belonged to my father. His name is marked on its edge." She narrowed her eyes at him. "But why would it be hidden beneath the floorboard in your bedchamber?"

"I was hoping Lotharian might be able to enlighten us. For it is plain that he knew it was there." Laird nailed the old man with a steely gaze.

"On my honor, I did not know it was there." Lotharian's piercing gray eyes stared back at Laird.

"Do you take me for a fool, Lotharian?" Laird took a step toward the man, hoping to intimidate him. Lord Lotharian was tall and broad-shouldered, much like Laird himself. But the years had dissolved what muscles might once have defined his flesh, and physically, Lotharian was no longer a threat. But the old man was shrewd, a gambling legend at White's and Boodle's. "You broke into my home through my bedchamber window, opened the floorboard, and stole the blade."

Apsley sniggered at that. "Well, obviously he knew *something* was there. The ivory is all he managed to retrieve, it seems."

"He didn't know the blade was there, didn't know anything about it." Elizabeth rolled her eyes in frustration. "He thought, we all thought, that *letters* were hidden beneath the floorboard." Realizing her faux pas, Elizabeth slapped her palm to her mouth and said nothing more.

"Letters? What letters?" Laird glanced from one person to the next to find his answer, but only blank expressions met his questioning gaze. He softened his gaze and turned to Anne. "Miss Royle, will you tell me?"

Anne walked slowly from before the hearth to

stand beside Laird. "Letters to Maria Fitzherbert—from the Prince of Wales."

Lady Upperton gasped. "No, dear! Say no more."

"No, I think he must know. After all, he is bound to hear society's whispers if he has not already." Anne raised her chin, the adorable way he noticed she always did before saying something bolder than was true to her nature. "The Old Rakes are convinced that your father had taken possession of several letters the Prince of Wales had written to Maria Fitzherbert when the two were separated for a time early in their relationship."

Laird huffed a laugh at that, but no one joined in his amusement. "Why would my father possess these letters? The notion is utterly ridiculous! It is common knowledge that the Prince Regent hated my father with a passion."

"Because, lad, it was not always so. Like Lotharian, Gallantine, and I, your father was once an intimate of Prinny's." Lilywhite lifted his glass to his lips and sipped a bit of brandy, as if he were bracing himself—or perhaps waiting for someone else to say something more.

That was Gallantine. "It's true. Your late father

was once Prinny's closest friend. So completely faithful that he was entrusted with couriering the prince's most private words to his secret Catholic wife, Maria Fitzherbert. Until, some say, his ambition got the better of him, and rather than delivering some of Prinny's letters to Maria, he pocketed them. Rumor is, he hid them away to use as leverage within Parliament. I daresay there are those who believe the accusation to be fact as opposed to innuendo. This, I fear, might have marked the beginning of the rift between the prince and your father."

Laird's swig of brandy seemed to drain from his mouth and into his lungs instead of his belly, sending forth a hail of coughs. "Wh-what madness is this?"

"Sit down, MacLaren. This is quite a lot to digest." Lotharian waved Lilywhite back from the chair opposite Aunt Prudence, and gestured for Laird to be seated. "You were not aware of any of this, my lord?"

Laird shook his head. None of this made any sense to him. This had to be a mistake.

"Your father did the prince a great service once, something that might have endeared him to the Crown for life." Lotharian caned his way to the settee and took his place beside Lady Upperton. "Do you wish to hear of this? I will tell you now, though when I have finished, your view of your late father may change—and not for the better."

"I do wish it." Laird leaned forward, resting his elbows on his knees, reluctant to miss a moment of this unbelievable revelation. "Tell me."

Lotharian nodded, and once the butler refilled his glass, he continued. "When the king was enduring his first prolonged delinquency of the mind—"

"He went *mad*," Lady Upperton clarified.

"Now then, I was saying . . . Pitt, the prime minister, succeeded in muting the seriousness of the king's condition to protect his place in Parliament."

Lady Upperton waved a finger in the air. "He covered it up! Had one of the doctors write optimistic accounts of his progress, rather than report the truth."

Lotharian groaned. "Your father sided with the Whig leader, Charles James Fox, whose own strength in the House was growing. Soon MacLaren and Fox became a driving force in convincing Parliament to vote to present a bill to make the Prince of Wales regent."

"Oh, do let us speak plainly," Lady Upperton suggested. "He and Fox *bribed* them, though publicly the money was issued as pensions and gifts."

"Eh . . . thank you, Lady Upperton," Lotharian murmured. "Prinny made it clear to Fox and your father that he wished to publicly declare his marriage to Maria Fitzherbert, a Catholic. As long as the king ruled, however, this was an impossibility. But if Parliament could pass a bill that would transfer rule to the prince, the prince thought he might be able admit his marriage to Maria."

Lady Upperton broke in again. "Of course, this would never happen, because if the prince's illegal marriage to Maria Fitzherbert was exposed, the nation would have been scandalized."

"Exactly," Gallantine said, while madly scratching his forehead beneath his wig. "Any parliamentary proposal to aid the prince would have been doomed. But with the prince made regent, Fox's and your father's influence in Parliament would be boundless—their futures assured."

"I think this was all the motivation they needed," Lotharian added, reclaiming the conversation. "Somehow, the evidence that Pitt claimed to possess that exposed the prince's secret marriage *disappeared*. Fox proclaimed the story of marriage a calumny. And eventually, due in large part to your father's efforts, a bill appointing the Prince Regent was passed shortly thereafter."

"Do you mean to tell me that my father was responsible for transferring rule from the king to the Prince of Wales?" Laird was flabbergasted.

"Well, yes, in great part. But he did so with the utmost secrecy." Gallantine slid his auburn wig back farther on his visibly sweating head. "What he, and Fox of course, achieved was no less than miraculous. Pitt and his supporters had fought long and hard to maintain the king's image and strengthen their position in Parliament," Gallantine explained. "But your father's cleverness and ingenuity tipped the balance in the prince's favor."

Apsley walked to the mantel and leaned against it. "But Prinny never did declare his marriage to Maria Fitzherbert."

"No, he didn't," Miss Anne answered for

Gallantine. "He was a weak man, and folded to pressure to marry another in exchange for payment of his debts."

Anne looked straight into Laird's eyes. "This is why those letters or whatever evidence your father possessed are so very important."

"I don't understand." Laird looked up at Apsley, sure that somehow he had missed something.

"Gorblimey!" Apsley suddenly focused his gaze upon the Royle sisters, and then exclaimed, "You're those chits! Remember? I told you on our walk here that her name sounded so familiar to me."

Elizabeth made her way to Anne and held her hand for support.

"Do you know who they are? They're the *Royle sisters*." Apsley grew more and more excited as he waited for Laird to make some connection. But none was to be had.

"I have been in mourning for my brother . . . and father for a year, Apsley. I have been in St. Albans, in the country, not in London. So if there is something I should know about the Royle family, do tell me."

"Good God, MacLaren! Only the juiciest bit

of society gossip to touch the lips of London's Quality." His eyes were wide. "Miss Anne and Miss Elizabeth, they are—"

But it was Anne who completed Apsley's sentence. "It has been rumored that Maria Fitzherbert was once with child. There are indications that my sisters and I are *possibly* the results of her confinement. *Triplets*. The secret daughters of the Prince of Wales and Maria Fitzherbert."

Laird stared at Anne. The claims he was hearing in this household grew more outlandish by the minute. "But if you are the prince's daughters, that would mean, by blood at least, you are—"

"*Princesses*." Lady Upperton beamed excitedly. "Yes! So now you understand why those letters are so important to us all."

This was all too much to absorb in his mind. *Bloody hell*. Just whom had he involved himself with last night?

Or had Apsley gotten it right when he suggested that the sisters and the Old Rakes had targeted him? Could they have deceitfully and purposely woven their way into his life?

No, no. This was all too outrageous to believe. All of it.

Laird's temples began to throb painfully, and he raised his glass to MacTavish. "Do pour me another brandy, man. Please, hurry." Then suddenly he flipped his wrist and halted the butler. "No, wait."

"Aye, my lord." The butler settled the bottle of swirling amber spirits back to his salver. "Have you changed your mind about a glass of brandy, sir?"

"I have. Just bring me the whole damned decanter."

Chapter 7

How to Remove Tarnish

"**O**h no," Anne muttered to herself. No more delays. She could not bear waiting any longer to be gifted with the details of her fate as a betrothed woman.

Lurching forward, she managed to intercept MacTavish's dutiful delivery of the brandy decanter. Then, with a firm grip, she ringed its cut-crystal neck between her index finger and thumb and settled it atop the tea table. "Lord MacLaren, far be it from me to deny a guest a libation," she said, "but we still have so much to discuss. I gather that the stories you have heard this night about your father may have been largely unknown to you, but you, my lord, possess information that is still unknown to me. I would be most pleased if you would share it."

"I beg your pardon, Miss Anne." The earl appeared confused, but, la, he was not fooling her. He knew exactly to what she referred.

"Oh botheration." Elizabeth folded her hands across her chest. "She wants the hideous details of your betrothal."

"Ah, yes. That."

"Lord MacLaren, I do not wish to delay our discussion another day. Waiting all day and half the evening for you to arrive was vexing enough." Anne crumpled a handful of her skirts in her fist. "So, since I know how important it is that your mind remain clear before discussing such matters, perhaps you would care for a dish of Bohea tea instead, hmm?"

The earl momentarily rested his forehead in his hand, and she could have sworn she heard him groan softly. "I do admit my mind was wholly distracted upon hearing of my father's past deeds." He turned his piercing cobalt-blue eyes from Anne to Lotharian.

The earl's lips seemed to thin, and for the first time, Anne began to doubt the wisdom of divulging his father's involvement in the mystery of her heritage.

"While the specifics of my father's unyielding

drive to succeed in Parliament are unsettling," Lord MacLaren somehow managed to say without moving his lips hardly at all, "I do not question your account, sir. Not in the least. My family has long suffered my father's lofty political ambitions and his willingness to sacrifice *anyone* and anything to achieve them."

Apsley expelled a nervous laugh at the earl's comment. "Well, well, let us not dwell on the past, I always say. You know, I believe I am still chilled from our walk to Berkeley Square. Aren't you, MacLaren?" Apsley made a show of rubbing his hands before an invisible fire in the cold hearth as if to warm them. "I agree with you wholeheartedly, Miss Royle. Tea would be just the thing to warm our bodies. Thank you."

There was a clatter of china in the passage, and Anne looked up just as Cherie, the silent maid-of-all-things, appeared in the parlor doorway with a tray filled with a steaming pot of tea, biscuits, linens, and dainty blue and white teacups.

MacTavish hobbled over to the tiny maid, took the tray from her, and began to lay the tea table for service.

Anne never ascertained how the wordless

maid always seemed to know the family's desires or wants before the wish was spoken, but somehow she did. This seemingly preternatural ability to anticipate, coupled with her silent, gentle manner, quickly had made her an essential member of the household staff.

Before quitting the room, Cherie stepped forward, luring Anne's eye back to her. The maid directed her gaze to the cup separated from the others. Anne peered down and saw the teacup with a tiny crack sloping down from the lip. She would be sure to take that cup, and obscure from the earl's notice her family's need to economize whenever possible.

She nodded her thanks to Cherie, and then, as the eldest able member of the family present, Anne took on the role of Mother, and began to pour the tea. Her hand shook slightly, sending the teacup rattling on its dish when it came time for her to serve the Earl of MacLaren.

He reached out as if to take the dish of tea from her, but instead guided her hand and the jiggling teacup to the tray. When she set it down, she raised her eyes to his.

"Honestly, Miss Anne, there is only one thing I require of you," he said softly, the talk of his father having drained the fight from his limbs and vinegar from his lips. "Grant me just a few minutes of privacy, if you please, so that we may discuss, as you have requested, the terms of our betrothal. I do not wish for you to be vexed any longer."

"Oh. Right, then." Anne nodded in assent, and after excusing herself from the gathering, led the earl down the dark passageway to the library.

The library door was already open and the flicker of candles softly illuminated the book-filled cases lining the walls. A newly lit coal fire burned in the grate, urging a tiny smile to Anne's lips. Cherie had been here, likely even before tending to the tea.

"Miss Anne," the earl began, the precise moment she opened her mouth to offer him a chair. "Let me begin by asking that you avoid spending any time alone with my mother."

"Your mother? I do not understand."

"We cannot allow her to learn your true reason for entering my bedchamber. Though I had my differences with my father, I wish to preserve her loving image of her husband. Hearing of his political ploys would destroy her memory of him." Laird raised his hand to stop the string of questions he obviously anticipated from her. "I vow, it will not be an easy to task to evade Lady MacLaren's company. She is already very curious about you, and is quite formidable. She will wish to know you much better and most assuredly will take it upon herself to teach and guide you in the most effective ways to establish a place for yourself within society."

Anne gestured to a chair near the hearth, but he paid her hospitality no heed. His eyebrows were drawn close, and he began to nervously pace the length of the Turkey carpet, giving her yet another glimpse of broad shoulders.

Lud, what did he need to admit that had him so agitated? Anne warily eased into a companion chair and sent her gaze trailing after him.

Well, now. His tailor was clearly quite good, she decided, for his coat was perfectly fitted to hug his muscular form. As were his breeches. Splendidly done. Why, she could not tell if the definition in his thigh muscles was truly just that, or a clever trick courtesy of his tailor. Of course, he had been blessed with a fair form. No question about that. Still, well done. Well done, indeed.

"Miss Anne?"

She looked up. Lord MacLaren had stopped pacing and was just standing there, looking at her.

"Yes, my lord?"

"Is there something amiss?" He glanced down and checked the fastening of the buttons at the fall of his breeches.

"Why no, my lord." Anne redirected her gaze to her hands for a moment, hoping, rather ridiculously she supposed, that perhaps he didn't notice her . . . er . . . appreciation of his tailor's skill.

When she looked up at him again, she saw that his dark eyebrows were cinched, as if they were determined to meet at the bridge of his nose.

Criminy. Anne shrugged. "You have seen through me, I was lost in my own fretful thoughts. I do beg your pardon, Lord MacLaren."

"*Laird*, please." The earl exhaled. "When my father died, we were estranged. Every time I hear 'Lord MacLaren,' I feel it as surely as a slap to my cheek. So please, at least when we are alone . . . *Laird*."

Laird. Strong. A leader. Rugged.

Oh, the name fit him as perfectly as his clothing. Defined him so well. But, la, she felt almost wicked using his Christian name. Unless . . . its use was a trade.

She looked up at him through her lashes, feeling oddly coquettish. "Perhaps, if you call me Anne. Agreed?"

"Agreed." But then a crooked grin curved his lips. "Though, after you hear the terms of betrothal, I shall not blame you too much if you call me any number of more colorful names."

Anne shuddered inwardly, reminding herself that he was a rake—and rakes could never be trusted. "My lord—"

"No, lass," he said in a most affected brogue. "Weave a wee bit more Scots into your pronunciation. *Laird*, not lord." He waved at her as if he wished her to stand, or something. "You try it now. Go on. *My Laird* . . ."

Heat flooded Anne's face. She swallowed deeply and forced herself to ignore his rakish game and continue with what she had planned to say. "*Laird*, I do not possess a flair for the stage. I loathe attention. It frightens me. And what you ask of me . . . well, I am not sure I can carry it off."

"And yet you have already charmed your audience." He strode back across the library and came down on his knee before her. "*Anne.*"

Good heavens. A wild jolt streamed through her limbs. He was not going to truly ask for her hand in marriage, was he? All to avoid disgracing his mother?

No, this was too much. Her legs twitched, and Anne twisted in the chair, thinking she might slip past him.

He saw her intent too quickly and slapped a hand to each of chair's arms, effectively preventing any escape.

"Why the ruse?" she whimpered. "I understand your desire to protect your mother from the embarrassment of our sham of an engagement—"

He was shaking his head, and for some reason, Anne found herself focusing on the cleft in his chin.

"I do wish to protect her," he was saying. "She has endured enough. But I ask you to pose as my betrothed *for me*. No one else."

In the haloed golden candlelight of the library, dust motes rode the air like fireflies in the night.

Even Anne's eyes sparkled like a gilt frame rounding a looking glass, reflecting only the darkness of his coat. Her chest rose and fell, and it required all of Laird's presence of mind to hold only her gaze, and not her person.

He thought just a moment ago, when he caught the armrests of the chair, that his sudden closeness disturbed her. Now he was not so convinced, for the rosy flush in her cheeks just now urged him to reexamine his hasty conclusion.

"What do you mean, *for you*?" Her voice was thin and breathy, and he felt his gaze dipping to her mouth.

Then the irony of the moment struck him coldly.

Here he was, desiring nothing beyond pressing his lips to this beautiful, utterly fascinating paradox of a woman . . . when he was about to beseech her to help him win the hand of another woman.

Abruptly Laird pushed back from the chair, rocked onto his heels, and came to his feet. He stepped toward the mantel, feeling unable, at that moment, to face her.

He knew she only agreed to remain betrothed until the end of the season because he was forcing her. It was not the gentlemanly thing to do. He'd sworn that he would change, become a better man, and he had over the past year, more or less. This evening, definitely less.

He'd seized the opportunity the moment he spied the Old Rakes in his garden in shackles. Like Lotharian, he was a consummate gambler, and knew that on occasion it was worth the risk of three spades of rank to open the queen of hearts to play.

Laird drew a breath deep into his lungs and willed himself to turn and meet her gaze as he spoke. "Anne, the Laird Allan who left London more than a year ago was exactly as you heard: a cad, a blackguard, and a Lothario of the worst sort. He cared nothing for the women whose hearts, and sometimes reputations, he had shattered. He had been shallow, had thought only of himself and his own pleasure. He'd enjoyed gaming, wicked games of the mind, but most of all, he'd reveled in humiliating his father, the censorious Earl of MacLaren, before his peers."

Anne tilted her head and seemed to study him for some seconds before speaking. "I do not understand. You said you knew how important his standing in the House of Lords was to him. Why would you seek to humiliate him?"

"Yes, I knew. I think I mentioned, too, that we

were estranged." Laird coughed a short laugh to break the emotional wedge that had risen in his throat. "As a lad, I never managed to meet the lofty expectations he had placed on his heir. He told me so, again and again. By time I was at Oxford, I had given up. I no longer tried to earn his praise and respect. In fact, I did the opposite. I did my damnedest to excel at exactly what repulsed him most. I drank and gambled heavily. I even wooed the wives of his peers, all to humiliate him. And, fancy that, I did very well."

"I'm confused why you are confiding in me about this." Anne came to her feet and implored him, "Please, just tell me what you expect of me."

"I am getting to that." Christ, he wished she would stop looking at him like that, all innocence and delicacy, when he knew, from her willingness to slip into his own bedchamber to steal from him, that she was not nearly as guileless as she pretended. "My ill reputation was well deserved. I freely admit that fact."

She sighed at what she clearly perceived as another delay to his revelation of terms. "Hardly a secret, Laird. All of London knows as much."

"Exactly. After a time, my antics no longer

seemed to irritate my father. And truth to tell, his approval, or rather lack of it, no longer seemed to matter to me. I was a man, no longer a boy needing a pat on the head. So I vowed to put my wicked ways behind me. To marry, and to live the rest of my days as a good and respectable man—like my brother, Graham."

Bloody hell. This was too damned hard. Laird looked around the room. "Any brandy about?"

Anne crossed her arms beneath her breasts. "You do not need a libation. You need to finish confessing whatever it is that you must, and then tell me what is required of me!"

Laird exhaled. "Getting there."

"But not quickly enough. *Please.*"

She was right about his need for confession. Laird needed to tell someone all this. He just didn't know why, after all these years of walling it up inside him, he needed *Anne* to be his confessor.

"But as you said, Anne, my black reputation was well known by every proper lady of Quality. But then, when in St. Albans, I met a widow, Constance, Lady Henceforth."

"And you offered for her, and she accepted, but cried off . . . when somehow she learned of your past." Anne's eyes brightened, and she took a step toward him. "Am I correct?"

"Yes, she is the woman who left me standing at the altar, alone." Laird closed the space between them and grasped Anne's shoulders gently, unintentionally sending the cool blue silk sleeves of her gown sliding down her arms, ever so slightly. He heard her gasp. "I-I didn't mean to . . ."

Or did he? He'd done just the same thing to so many women, he honestly did not know just then if it really was an accident, or if the rake inside him wanted it.

Anne reached up with both her hands, removed his palms from her shoulders, and tugged the sleeves back atop them as best she could. "Think nothing of it. The dress has been slipping all eve." Then, as if to reestablish the distance between them, she turned and started for the door.

"Wait!" He reached a hand out to her, but his fingers closed only on air. "I haven't told you what I require."

Anne halted and looked back at him over her pale shoulder. "Yes, you did." Her body turned until it aligned with the angle of her head. "You want me to redeem you—to restore your respectability."

Nerves fired, shaking Laird's body. "Not quite the words I was expecting to hear."

"But I speak the truth, do I not?" Anne lifted her golden eyebrows and waited for his response.

Laird sighed. "Yes."

"And once society deems you are respectable, a man of honor, then I am free to cry off. Do I have the right of it?"

"Society must be convinced that I am a changed gentleman, one worthy of taking my father's seat in the House of Lords, certainly. But I do not do this to prove worthiness to the *ton*."

"Then for whom do you wish this? Your mother? I know wiping away the tarnish from your reputation is important to her." Anne lifted her eyebrows and waited expectantly for his reply.

"I do it for Lady Henceforth, and once she believes I am honorable and good, I will be in need of that ring on your finger."

"So all I have to do is help you prove to the world that you have changed—that you have become a bona fide gentleman. Then I can claim that, though you are a good man, a worthy man, I cannot marry you because I do not love you."

"Or some other way of crying off that does not attribute blame to either one of us, yes." Laird's gaze was unyielding as he awaited her agreement with his plan.

Anne folded her arms at her chest and sighed heavily. "You wish me to do this so that Lady Henceforth will see you in a more flattering light and will accept your betrothal ring?"

"Yes." Laird dropped his gaze momentarily to the floor while he anxiously awaited her reply.

"Well, if that it all there is to it, I'll ready the boning knife." Anne smiled mischievously at him, then turned and walked into the passageway.

Chapter 8

How to Coax an Invitation

Cockspur Street

Laird had inherited a number of valuables from his late father. Among them, his elegant town house on Cockspur Street; two fine portraits by George Romney, both of exceedingly beautiful women (who, not surprisingly, had at one time been mistresses of the Prince of Wales); a clan property in the Highlands of Scotland; a crumbling country estate in St. Albans, and a collection of ancient maps from the Crusades.

But Laird treasured none of these things more than he valued Rupert Festidious, the butler, who, oddly enough, seemed to convey with the town house on Cockspur after the Earl of MacLaren, the elder, passed away.

The residence on Cockspur was ideally suited to a bachelor. It was conveniently located at the end of Pall Mall, only one minute's walk from the lovely dancers at the Opera House, or four minutes from drink and gaming at White's.

Given what he had learned the night before, Laird supposed that his father likely appreciated the fact that Prinny's residence, Carlton House, was located but a breath away as well. At least he might have, before the prince became regent. Sometime after that momentous day, Laird was sure his father rued the now-uncomfortable proximity.

The butler, Festidious, was likely unaware of the benefits of the house's prime location. He rarely left the premises, due, Laird surmised, to worry that the house staff might run amok and embarrass him by failing to polish the silver properly or leaving wrinkles in the bed linens. But Laird rather liked this about the butler.

In Laird's opinion, Festidious's lofty standards of service were unsurpassed, and the smooth running of the Cockspur household seemed a great point of pride for the elderly butler.

The house was always stocked with good brandy, wine, and tea. The meals he planned with Cook were delicious and unique, without being excessively dear to the pocket. The staff admired the butler and seemed to work hard to earn his nod.

Laird could not surmise how his late father, being such a cold and selfish man, could have earned the butler's loyalty. It was evident, however, that he had. Laird planned to do the same and to do whatever was required of him to ensure that Festidious remained in his employ.

So, when Festidious informed the new earl that the staff had spent the entire day conducting a thorough search of the house and no letters of any sort were found, hidden or otherwise, Laird believed him implicitly.

However, he also believed Lotharian.

He did not doubt for one instant that his father had, at least at one time, possessed the letters the Old Rakes had described last night. Or that the old earl had possibly tried to leverage whatever information was contained within their text to garner some sort of political gain from the prince.

It would have been a daring game that his father played, to be sure. One that, given the evidence of his reduction in influence in the House of Lords over his lifetime, had somehow gone awry.

His father's ill-conceived scheme mattered not a bit to Laird, however. The fact that the letters were no longer in the house, however, *did* matter.

This fact propelled Laird into his study.

He would send a message to Anne at once to let her know. Maybe a missive to the Old Rakes might be in order as well to put an end to any more nocturnal invasions by elderly men garbed in black.

Sliding open the desk drawer, Laird withdrew a sheet of foolscap, a quill pen, and a pot of ink, and sat down to write.

Anne wouldn't be pleased with the news. She truly wished to find evidence to support or disprove the claim that she and her sisters were born blue-blooded. But at the moment, Laird was just feeling incredibly fortunate that the letters containing proof were not to be found at Cockspur. Oh, he was not so cocksure to presume that this small blessing vindicated his father from the crime of which the Old Rakes had accused him. It only meant that there was no evidence at Cockspur to directly prove his complicity.

Laird closed his fingertips tightly around the nib end of the quill pen, unconsciously staining them with ink, as he pondered the wording of his note.

Anne was a shrewd woman, and she would immediately detect any hint of subterfuge in his inked words.

He had to be careful. Very careful.

She needed to believe that he had ordered the town house searched from kitchen to attic, and that every crack and nook, every mouse hole and chimney flue, had been thoroughly probed—*for her*.

Not to conceal evidence of his father's possible act of treason. Not to protect his mother or the family name from scandal.

For her.

Laird glanced through the study window at the fading evening light. It was not so late. And the more he considered the importance of his phrasing, the more convinced he became that putting the outcome of the search in writing was not a wise idea.

He could wheel over to Berkeley Square and tell Anne himself. As the idea swelled, he absently nodded his head. Yes, telling her in person was the more gentlemanly route anyway.

He strode across the drawing room and was just leaning his head into the passage to call for his carriage when Festidious appeared as if from nowhere.

"Damn me, man. You startled at least a year off my life!"

"I beg your pardon, my lord." The balding butler did not meet Laird's startled gaze, but stared straight ahead.

"Will you call for my carriage, please? I should like to go to Berkeley Square."

"I do apologize, my lord, but your mother has taken the carriage. I shall send a footman to hail a hackney for you at once."

Laird peered down at the rigid butler. Gorblimey, did the man ever blink? "Lady MacLaren has taken the carriage without a word to me? Where has she gone?"

"Begging your forgiveness, my lord, I had no knowledge that you would wish to go to Berkeley Square as well. I should have confirmed your schedule with you. Again, I do apologize."

Laird squinted down at the butler. "Are you telling me my mother is in Berkeley Square?"

"Yes, my lord. She left shortly after Sir Lumley Lilywhite visited earlier today."

"Lilywhite?" *Anne's guardian?* This did not bode well.

"Yes, my lord. Berkeley Square was Lady Mac-Laren's destination. That is what . . . what she *said.*"

"What do you mean by that, Festidious? Is there any reason you would doubt her?"

"No, my lord, certainly not. 'Tis just I found it rather curious that she had a portmanteau packed atop the cab, and that she brought her lady's maid with her . . . to Berkeley Square."

Damn it all. Laird had no idea what to make of this. It was odd enough by half, even for his mother. "B-by any chance, Festidious, do you know if it was her intention to call on Miss Anne Royle?"

"I believe she mentioned Miss Royle, yes, my lord." The butler stared blankly past Laird's head as though he were a blind man or address-ing the regent himself. "Shall I call for a hackney then, my lord?"

"Devil's balls!" Laird shoved his hands through his hair. "No time. Have my horse brought 'round. Hurry now!"

There was no way he could allow his mother to be alone with Anne.

Too many damning secrets could slip. Secrets he had not even had just one day before.

Berkeley Square

When the butler MacTavish announced Laird and led him into the parlor, it was as he feared; neither Anne nor his mother was present.

Miss Elizabeth and Mrs. Winks, the Royle sisters' ever-sleeping aunt, were surrounded by Lady Upperton and the three Old Rakes.

"They've already gone, dear boy," Lotharian droned, though a slight hint of a smile was tugging at his mouth. "Left an hour ago. The weather is fair; the roads dry. Surely they are halfway to St. Albans. You won't catch them up now."

"I don't understand." Laird turned the rim of his glossy beaver hat around in his hands. "You know our betrothal is naught but a sham. If she spends any time alone with my prying mother, Anne's true reason for slipping into my bedchamber will eventually be revealed—to the detriment of us all. It might already be too late."

Laird began to pace before the parlor door. "Why was Anne permitted to leave with her?"

"No one *permitted* her, my lord. She went because she knew she must—because the letters were not at Cockspur," Lilywhite informed him. "The next logical location to search would be your family estate, MacLaren Hall. Surely you realize that, MacLaren."

Laird stilled his step and whipped his head around to face Sir Lumley. "But I hadn't yet mentioned—"

"The letters?" Elizabeth broke in. "Yes, we already know about the unsuccessful search. I suspect we did before you yourself were told." Miss Elizabeth crossed the parlor and led Laird by his elbow to her own seat on the settee next to Lady Upperton.

"But how?" Laird asked the young woman.

Though he expected that Elizabeth would take her ease in another chair, she remained standing before him. "It was Mrs. Polkshank, our cook. At our urging, she forged . . . a new friendship at Cockspur."

"Oh, go ahead and say it, Elizabeth," Lotharian complained. "I paid Mrs. Polkshank to ensure that word would be sent to the Old Rakes of Marylebone if a search for the letters was conducted, or if they were found by you or a member of your staff. "

"But the letters were not found."

"No, the search you organized was fruitless. But very helpful to us indeed." Lotharian tipped his head at Laird. "And for that, we thank you, my lord."

Lady Upperton patted Laird's forearm in that placating manner older women have. "Since the letters were not at your residence in Cockspur, we concluded that your father likely would have hidden them somewhere at MacLaren Hall."

Lilywhite tugged at his lapel, and his mouth angled proudly. "I vow, I must be more charming than I know. It took nothing to convince your mother to take Anne to MacLaren Hall with her immediately."

"So urging my mother to take Anne to St. Albans was your reason for calling at Cockspur?" Laird shook his head. He didn't need to hear Lilywhite's reply. Of course it was.

"Well, during our most delightful conversation about the upcoming nuptials, I might have let it slip that Anne is somewhat unschooled in the ways of polite society. And that I would be eternally grateful for any guidance Lady Mac-Laren could lend our gel. In the end, I think she fancied it her own idea."

"Sir Lumley, while I do not doubt your *charm* with the ladies, I am quite sure that my mother invited Anne to MacLaren Hall because it was her plan all along. She admitted she was horrified by the harum-scarum way our betrothal was announced. She will not abide another social embarrassment." Laird sighed and closed his eyes. It was all too clear now. "What better way to ensure that than to whisk Anne to the country to instruct her in what will be expected from her as my intended."

"It doesn't really matter. Anne is a very clever woman. She will do whatever your mother wishes. But make no mistake, Lord MacLaren, she is there for one reason only—to search for the letters. And that, young man, is exactly what she will do."

Laird shot to his feet. "I can't believe Anne agreed to do this. She claimed posing as my betrothed was beyond her abilities."

Elizabeth was shaking her head. "My lord, until a year ago, my sisters and I believed we were left on a country doctor's doorstep by some poor unfortunate soul. Anne has never known her family, her history," Elizabeth said.

"I don't understand what you mean."

"As a child, being so shy and awkward, she was teased and ridiculed by the other children from the village. To avoid this, she learned to remain on the fringes and to avoid doing anything that would bring her notice."

"And yet she left with my mother."

"Only because her desire to know, at last, who she is exceeds her fear of attention." Elizabeth reached out and squeezed his hand in hers. "Unless you know what it is like to be raised without roots, without respectability, Lord MacLaren, please, do not judge her for what you can never understand."

Laird stood there silently for several moments before quitting the room to make his way to St. Albans.

Elizabeth had been right on one point—Laird had never known what it was to live without roots. He had only to look up at the gallery walls at MacLaren Hall to see the Allan bloodline.

But if there was one thing he did know something about, it was living without respectability.

And, sadly, he knew the aching desperation of it as well.

Laird mounted his horse and set his heels to its haunches. He had to reach Anne before she did something she'd later come to regret.

Cavendish Square
Later that night

"I tell you both, the letters we seek *were* in the house, probably still are." Lotharian paced the library, pausing before a shelf of books. Absently he ran his fingers across the polished leather spines, as if browsing, with no particular title in mind.

"What makes you so sure, my lord?" Elizabeth toyed with the workings of Lady Upperton's mechanical tea server, while the older woman positioned the cups to receive the steaming brew.

Before Lotharian could answer, the cool air in the room rushed across the library, as the seal of the secret door in the bookcases was broken and the door pivoted open.

Lotharian withdrew a handkerchief from his coat and wiped the thin coating of oil from his fingertip. He turned, and along with Lady Upperton and Elizabeth, waited as Lilywhite and Gallantine shuffled across the library and took their chairs. "I was just telling Elizabeth that the letters were in MacLaren's Cockspur Street town house, and recently, too. The search of the house had to have produced something."

"How are you so sure, Lotharian?" Lady Upperton flipped the lever, and the tea server began to click and roll toward the cups.

Elizabeth's eyes widened, and she bent until her nose was even with the edge of the tea table to watch as the server tilted and began to pour the first dish of tea. "MacLaren had the house searched, and rake or not, he does not seem to be the sort who would lie about such a thing."

"No, he is not a liar. That much I am sure of," Lotharian said, "but the letters were in the house—at least until the week before the younger MacLaren opened the house for the season."

Elizabeth sat upright and accepted a dish of tea from Lady Upperton. "I remember Apsley saying as much . . . the night you three were discovered dangling by ropes from MacLaren's rooftop." She giggled quietly into her tea.

Lilywhite lifted his thick eyebrows. "That doesn't prove the letters were still there. It only proves that the men breaking into the house, assuming they were the same crew, either didn't find the letters the first time or they were never looking for the letters. Every newspaper in Town touted the MacLaren rout marking the family's return to London. It is a fair assumption that the burglars deduced that since the family was returning to London, they weren't bloody well there yet, and that the house would be unoccupied and ripe for the plucking."

Gallantine cleared his throat. "Except, Lilywhite, for the second time, nothing of notice was reported missing."

"The elder MacLaren surprised them the first time, and Apsley the second." Lilywhite took a cup of tea from Lady Upperton and sniffed it. "My dear lady, have you a splash of brandy?"

With a sigh of exasperation, Lady Upperton pulled the lever at the side of her seat, and a small tufted footstool shot out from beneath the settee. She settled her tiny feet on it and climbed down, then crossed the library to collect a decanter of brandy.

"Apsley is a long-nosed sort. I do not believe I trust him." Elizabeth extended a hand and helped Lady Upperton climb back onto the settee with the brandy. "Didn't he say there were papers everywhere when he entered into the town house? If he saw the letters, he might have read them and discovered their value." Her eyes rounded. "He might have taken them."

Lilywhite nodded and sighed with pleasure as Lady Upperton topped his cup with a measure of brandy.

"Perhaps, Elizabeth." Gallantine held his cup out to Lady Upperton for her to add a little spirits to his tea as well. "But more than likely, Anne has the right of it, and will find the letters at MacLaren Hall."

"Yes, I fear we have no choice but to wait and hope that Anne will be successful in her search." Lotharian extended his now empty teacup.

Elizabeth expelled the air in her lungs. She had never been much good at waiting, but since she came to London it had been all she seemed to do.

"More tea, Lotharian?" Lady Upperton gestured to the tea server, but the Old Rake waved off the silly notion.

"No, my dear." Lotharian fashioned a charming smile especially for her. "But my bones are still a bit stiff from dangling from the ropes. Some brandy, however, might be just the thing."

Chapter 9

How to Travel in Style

MacLaren Hall, St. Albans
Midnight

Viscount Apsley's carriage was far better fitted than the mail coach Laird had considered taking for the two-hour trip north to St. Albans. There were fewer stops, and it was more supremely equipped for comfort than any carriage he'd ever had the pleasure of riding inside.

And, as the elegant town carriage turned down the center of the poplar tree-lined drive to MacLaren Hall, Laird almost wished the journey was not at its end. He'd been positively pampered from the moment they'd left London. It was like traveling inside a wheeled gentlemen's club.

They drank choice brandy, supped on delicacies from the wicker food hamper, played cards, and smoked cheroots from the West Indies.

Laird was glad that Apsley had insisted he join him in finding a way to wrench Anne from his mother and whisk her back to London.

He'd had to sit for three hours, as Apsley bathed and conferred with his valet about the appropriate clothing required for a short stay in a country house. It was actually worth the wait—though he'd never admit this aloud; that would please Apsley far too much, and he couldn't have that.

No, the longer Apsley felt he owed him for this fiasco of a betrothal, the better.

The carriage circled around and drew to a bouncy halt before the huge double doors of MacLaren Hall. Two young footmen, rubbing the sleep from their eyes and shrugging their coats over their shoulders, hurried out to assist the coachman and groom with Laird's small leather bag and Apsley's huge portmanteau.

Laird grabbed Apsley's arm and eased him from the cab. "There you go. We're here now."

Apsley, deep in his brandy-induced stupor, groaned in response.

"But you must be quiet. It is late, and Lady MacLaren and Miss Royle will certainly be in their beds."

Apsley tried to nod his head, but instead his chin just rolled a few inches across his chest.

After depositing his wilted friend into the first vacant bedchamber he came upon, Laird started up the stairway to find his own bed at the far end of the upper hallway.

The passage was dark, but he'd spent most of his young life roaming MacLaren Hall, and did not require a candle to find his way. He knew every inch of the house and grounds as well as his own face.

He slowed his step as he passed Graham's bedchamber, God rest and keep his soul. He remembered the two of them racing through this door into the hallway, heading for the stairs. They would each mount a side of the grand staircase's banister, and in a sliding race to the bottom, would whoop and holler the names of their imaginary horses while their governess fretted and screeched . . . and their mother laughed until her sides ached.

The warm memory set a smile upon Laird's mouth, until he noticed a low flicker of firelight coming from beneath the door. His head was clouded with the dulling effects of the brandy, and without thinking, he opened the door. "Graham?" he whispered.

Someone stirred in the bed, drawing Laird closer. "Graham?" He stopped when he reached the tester and briskly rubbed his hands over his face.

What was he doing? What was he thinking?

Graham is dead. Dead.

Still, someone was sleeping in his brother's bed.

Without taking another step, he reached for the curtain covering the window and drew it back just enough to break the darkness. A finger of cool moonlight cut through the window and fell upon the sleeping figure in the bed.

Laird inhaled a deep breath.

Anne.

"Moonlight becomes you, my dear," he whispered so softly that had she awakened right then, she might have heard only a sigh. If it were possible, he found her even more beautiful, more ethereal in her sleep.

In the pale blue light, her skin was like porcelain; her pale hair flowed over her smooth, bared shoulder like liquid silver. He wanted nothing so much at that moment than to kiss her.

He could not help himself. Laird reached out his free hand and lightly trailed his fingertips through her hair, then across her cheek before finally sliding a single finger across her full lower lip.

She stirred then, and he snatched back his finger from her mouth. He released the pinch of curtain he held and silently backed away from the tester bed, before turning and darting through the open door and into the passage.

The first rays of daylight at last breached the wall of trees bordering the east lawn and streamed into the library, assisting Anne with her search.

Lady MacLaren had mentioned that her dear departed husband had spent much of his time in this very room when he was in residence—which was not nearly as frequently as she would have liked. So the library, Anne had decided as she shoved the pins into her hair early that morning, was the first place she ought to search for the hidden letters.

Before the sun reached the room, she'd paced

the floor, taking care to peel back the gold and crimson carpet and push down with her toes on any piece of parquet that might seem loose or damaged in any way.

She'd dropped to her knees and had pressed on the skirting-board to check for any hidden compartment, and ran her fingertips along the breaks between the lower portions of the book-cases looking for hidden doors à la Lady Upperton's secret library passage.

But now the light in the ornate room was sufficient to deepen her search, though she was all too aware that her time was growing dear.

She had taken the precaution of closing the library door against nosy maids and footmen, but soon enough Lady MacLaren's belly would rumble and nudge her down the stairs to break her fast.

Anne focused her attention on the grand mahogany desk before the huge French windows. She tugged on the brass pulls, but every drawer was locked.

Turning around, she dropped onto her bottom and lay down in the cavernous knee hole. If there was key hidden about, she reasoned, it would need to be close for convenience's sake—but hidden from view.

Her fingers probed the underside of the center desk drawer, feeling the splintery gaps beneath the braces, and between the dovetails that had loosened over the years.

Unexpectedly, a shadow passed between her and the window. She bent her neck and raised her head to peer up at the window, hoping that a cloud had only blocked the sun. But inside, she knew better.

Her stomach tensed as she squinted at the figure blocking her light.

Oh, perdition.

She'd been discovered.

Suddenly, large hands firmly gripped her ankles and yanked her out from beneath the desk. She lurched upright, hitting her forehead on the edge of the drawer molding.

"Blast!" she snapped, before looking up. She blinked at the hulking silhouette before the window.

"Watch out for the drawer," came Laird's amused voice. "Oh dear. Too late."

Anne ducked her head until she was past the drawer and sat up. She rubbed her smarting forehead, then cupped her hand to her brow, cutting the glare. "Wh-what are you doing here?"

154

"I was about to ask you the very same question." He was grinning at her instead of frightening her with his visual grimace. That was a good sign.

She flung a flailing hand in the air, which Laird grasped and used to haul her to her feet.

"Wh-why I was looking . . . for something to read," she replied with all the confidence she could muster.

"Under the desk?"

"I-I dropped your grandmother's ring." She quickly clapped her right hand over her left and began twisting. "Found it though. See?" She held up her left hand proudly.

"Hmm. Excuse me a moment, will you?" Laird leaned around her and took something from beneath the burl wood pen rest. He straightened. There was that grin again. "I thought you might be looking for *this*."

He opened his hand before her nose and showed her a shiny brass key.

Anne scowled. "If you knew what I was doing all along, why did you not just say so?"

"Now that wouldn't be half as amusing, would it?"

She folded her arms at her chest and gave her

head a haughty flick. "So you know why I have come."

"Yes, I do."

"You searched your town house in London for the letters, which I must say was very gracious of you." La, he was still grinning at her. "Perhaps you would condescend to assist me searching for them in here."

"No, I do not see the need." He shrugged his shoulders, almost mockingly to Anne's way of thinking, then strode across the room and leaned against the back of a large leather wingback chair.

"Do not see the need?" Anne flung her arms outward, but took care to keep her voice to a whisper. "How can you not? It makes perfect sense to me. If your father did indeed possess the letters, and they were not at Cockspur Street, then it is logical that he might have hidden them here."

"You are exactly right. *If* he ever possessed the letters, and we are not completely certain of that, then searching this library might be the thing to do right now—unless . . ."

"Unless what?"

"Unless *I* have already searched it."

"Searched it?" What was Laird on about? He was being nonsensical. "Impossible." She eyed him with suspicion. "Wh-when?"

"Last night," he replied smugly, "whilst you slept."

The library door flew open. Anne looked up to see Lady MacLaren standing in the doorway.

"Why, good morning, Lady MacLaren," Anne rushed to her and led her by the hand to Laird. "Look who has arrived. Is this not a wonderful surprise?"

Laird came around from the back of the chair and kissed the countess's cheek. "Oh, not such a surprise, was it, Mother?"

Lady MacLaren giggled like a girl. "No, I suppose not. I had a notion you might come once you learned I had taken Anne to MacLaren Hall."

"In *my* carriage," Laird added.

"Oh yes." Lady MacLaren's gaze plummeted to her feet. "How did you travel, dear? Your gelding?"

"Certainly not," came a chipper voice from the doorway. "He arrived in *my* carriage." Lord Apsley bowed in a most gentlemanly manner, and then in three long strides was standing among them. "Can't let our lad be all dust-packed when he is about to greet his mother and bride, now can we?"

Anne looked across at Laird. His left eyebrow was arched angrily and his vibrant blue eyes had narrowed at Apsley.

"Well then, we have the makings of a house party. Let us all take our morning tea together, shall we?" Lady MacLaren waved her arms as if to shoo them all toward the door.

"Yes, shall we, Anne?" Laird offered her his arm, which she grudgingly took.

Lady MacLaren evidently saw the uncomfortable exchange, and she questioned them immediately. "Why were the two of you in the library so early this morn?"

Anne laughed softly. "As it happened, we both awoke shortly before dawn and came upon each other in the library."

"We were both looking for something interesting to read," Laird added helpfully.

Lady MacLaren lifted her thin eyebrows. "And did either of you find it?"

"Not yet, Lady MacLaren, but then I do not think either of us is finished searching." Anne smiled prettily. "Are we, Lord MacLaren?"

"No, Anne." Laird's gaze fixed on her eyes. "We haven't finished . . . *yet*."

It seemed to Laird that his mother was in an extraordinarily bright mood this morning. She hummed through smiling lips as she topped a slice of toasted bread with a dollop of marmalade and chattered cheerfully with both Apsley and Anne as they all broke their fasts.

It was the first time he'd seen her this way, her former chipper self, since the report of Graham's death on the battlefield had arrived. It pleased Laird to see her happy again. Their small family had endured far too much pain over the past year and a half.

"Lady MacLaren, I must thank you for lodging me in such a warm and comfortable bedchamber." Anne's gaze flitted to Laird briefly. "But I have come to learn that this particular bedchamber is a family room, and I do not wish to impose." She glanced at Laird before facing Lady MacLaren for her reply.

"My dear gel, you are not imposing at all. And you are family, or soon will be." The countess patted Anne's shoulder. "Besides, I chose Graham's room for you myself."

"You did?" Laird stared at his mother in disbelief. For the entire year of mourning for her son, she had had the bedchamber cleaned as though Graham were coming home any day.

Though the countess never admitted it, Laird was of the belief that she never truly believed the report of his demise on the battlefield. Even when Graham's batman had come to return the signet ring that never left his brother's finger, Lady MacLaren still had the linens changed and a ewer of hot water set upon his washstand each night.

Until last night, it seemed.

"Yes, I did." The smile withered from Lady MacLaren's thin lips. "I could not abide seeing his bedchamber empty any longer." She turned and gazed at Anne, and her lips curved upward again. "But now Anne has joined us at MacLaren Hall. And soon we will all be a real family again—instead of a fragment of a family that once was happy here." Tears welled in his mother's eyes, not of sadness, but of happiness.

He heard a sniffle, and turned to see Anne dabbing her eyes. "Thank you, Lady MacLaren," she managed to say in a quavering voice through her tears. She leapt up from her chair and bent to hug

Lady MacLaren. "You do not know how much it means to hear you say this to me."

Laird felt heat at the backs of his eyes. Marrying Anne, in truth, would give her the roots she'd always longed for. And return to his mother the sense of family she'd lost after the deaths of Graham and her husband.

But he sought the affections of another, Lady Henceforth, and, as seemed to be his way, he would disappoint everyone. Once again.

Lady MacLaren suddenly clapped her hands, her eyes still wet with tears. "I have decided to take Anne into St. Albans with me this day. Who else will join us? We shall make a day of it."

Apsley stifled a yawn and blinked his red-laced, bleary eyes. "I do beg your pardon, Lady MacLaren, but I have yet to recover from our journey and might indulge myself with a few more minutes of rest, if you do not mind."

Laird grinned. More like to sleep off the brandy-induced pain in his head.

"Laird? What say you?" The countess smiled expectantly at him.

He pushed his chair back from the table and stood. "Actually, I had thought I might continue my search for something interesting to read, and then take a walk along the lake." He crossed to his mother and kissed her cheek. "Besides, I am sure you ladies will be shopping for ribbons and notions, and I have no talent for choosing such things. I will therefore leave you to enjoy each other's company. No doubt you have much to talk about."

He walked around the table to Anne and lowered his mouth to her ear. "Just not *too much*, darling, agreed?" he whispered.

Anne nodded her head, and then, for the notice of the others, she covered her mouth and giggled. "Oh, Laird, *behave*."

He lifted an eyebrow and winked. "Always, my dear."

Chapter 10

How to Be Patient

The village of St. Albans

Anne had always been the least patient of the three Royle sisters. Her father, who had to have been the most patient physician in all of England, had oft told her so. "Patience is a virtue," he counseled her whenever she was called upon to sit up all night with a feverish farmer or sick child.

So she silently reminded herself of the dictum during the minutes her sister Elizabeth stared down at the serving plate, trying to decide which bit of mutton she should choose for her supper.

And again she reminded herself while waiting three-quarters of an hour while her older sister,

Mary, dickered with a merchant over a penny she could save if she simply bought the tea from another shopkeeper.

So she waited, patiently, inside Laird's town carriage as Lady MacLaren had instructed. Truly, ever so patiently . . . until the bell in the town clock tower heralded the next hour.

It was then that Anne decided that something could be wrong. She really ought to check the health of Lady MacLaren, just to be certain she fared well.

Abruptly she flung open the carriage door, striking something. *Hard.*

A woman shrieked with pain.

"Oh, dear heavens, what have I done?" Anne leapt out of the carriage and slammed the door shut. There, a woman was sitting on the pavement, stunned. Blood gushed in streams from her pert little nose, staining her silk rose-striped walking ensemble.

"Oh, this is such a dreadful accident!" Anne rushed to her and dropped down at her side. "I am so sorry—I didn't see you coming." Anne tilted the woman's head back and pinched the bridge of her nose to slow the bleeding. Oh no. It moved. "I fear you have broken it, madam."

The woman whimpered. "You mean, *you* broke it."

"Yes, well, again, I do apologize. You cannot imagine how sorry I am for this."

"I saw the carriage . . . the MacLaren coat of arms on the door."

"Yes, that's right."

"But . . . what were you doing inside?" the woman managed between bloody snorts.

"I am Lord MacLaren's fiancée. Please, try not to speak. Do let me help you inside the apothecary until a physician can be summoned." Without awaiting a reply, Anne hoisted the woman to her feet.

The woman would not be led. "You are his betrothed? Laird Allan's?" At least, that was what Anne thought the woman was asking. It was hard to tell.

"Yes, I am. Please, madam, if you just come with me inside the shop, I know I can stop the bleeding."

"That is impossible." The woman suddenly became strangely calm.

"I assisted my father, a physician, my entire life. Truly, I can pack your nose and stop the bleeding." Anne tugged the woman toward the door.

"No, I mean it is impossible. Lord MacLaren becoming engaged again—so soon."

Anne was beginning to grow quite irritated with her patient. "Very well. Why is that?"

"Because he is just out of mourning."

"And how would you know that? Are you acquainted with the family?" Anne pushed the door ajar and held it open with the side of her slippered foot.

"Indeed, I am," the woman replied.

Lady MacLaren turned when the bell over the shop door sounded, as Anne yanked the woman inside the apothecary. Her bright smile trickled from her face. "Lady Henceforth!"

Lady Henceforth? A wave of sudden nausea shook Anne.

Please, someone tell me I did not just break the nose . . . of the woman who left Laird at the altar.

The sun had set by time the physician quit Lady Henceforth's bedchamber, only after securing a promise from Anne to watch over his patient until morning and to tend to her needs.

Lady MacLaren, who could not seem to abide the sight of the woman who had caused her son such disgrace, left the Henceforth house just as soon as she could return to MacLaren Hall.

Lady Henceforth swallowed deeply, sending a hail of blood-tinged coughs into her handkerchief and an abundance of tears into her eyes.

"There, there." Anne poured a glass of cool water and brought it to the woman's lips. "There is nothing to fear; you are not ill. You swallowed a goodly amount of the blood from your nose. Drink this down and help wash it from your throat."

"You . . . you are being so kind to me. Why, Miss Royle?"

"Please, call me Anne. Why wouldn't I help you? I did break your nose, Lady Henceforth." Anne smiled back at her.

"You may call me Constance." Then Lady Henceforth cast her teary brown eyes downward. "Because of what I did to Laird. Though I tell you in all truthfulness that I had to cry off. I had to. Once I learned what sort of man he was—a rake, a cad—I knew I could not spend my life with him."

"No need to explain yourself." Anne settled the glass on the table and patted Lady Henceforth's hand. "I do not judge you, dear lady."

"You are good, Anne." The words came almost as if Lady Henceforth was surprised to come to that conclusion. "How is it that you agreed to marry him? For his fortune? I cannot fathom any other reason why a woman such as yourself would bind herself to a man who will dishonor her as soon as the opportunity presents itself." A flat, oddly satisfied smile appeared on her lips.

"Dear lady!" Anne blinked with astonishment, and to her surprise, anger flared within her.

"I do apologize for being so blunt, but I could not bear it if I did not tell you." Lady Henceforth pulled Anne's hand toward her and clasped her other hand around it as well. "Perhaps you were not aware of his black reputation."

Anne steadied her breathing. *Do not react emotionally, no matter what Lady Henceforth says.*

After all, here was her first chance to fulfill her promise to Laird, and she had to take full advantage of it. "Constance, I live in London, and I am fully aware of Laird's history as the most wicked of rakes. But I assure you, Lord MacLaren is no longer that horrid man."

Lady Henceforth huffed at that. "A tiger cannot change its stripes."

"Nevertheless, after his father and brother died, Laird *did* change. He has reformed. He is a good and true man."

"So much in so short a time? I find that difficult to swallow."

Anne pulled her hand away and reached for the glass on the bedside table. "Perhaps some more water will help." She raised her eyebrows playfully, hoping to enliven Lady Henceforth's disposition.

She smiled and nestled against the pillows Anne had propped behind her back. "How did you meet? He is just out of mourning both his brother and his father."

Perdition. Why hadn't she and Laird discussed their meeting? It was wholly amazing no one had asked that question before! They always seemed too interested in the betrothal itself.

"Well, it is all quite unbelievable really." Anne took a sip of the water herself, hoping to purchase a bit more time. There was no possible way she could tell the truth; that was a given. "Well, I was walking along the banks of the Serpentine . . ."

And so began the second grandest lie of Anne's life.

* * *

The countess was quite calm and polite when she called upon Lady Henceforth the next morning. But once she had retrieved Anne and passed through the doors of MacLaren Hall, she grabbed Anne's hand and hustled her into the library without delay.

Laird looked up from his seat before the desk, then came directly to his feet. Anne was wearing the same cambric morning gown she had been wearing yesterday. Only now, blooms of dried blood marred the bodice and permanently streaked her skirt. "Are you all right? I was worried when you did not come home . . . I mean back."

Lady MacLaren could not contain herself. "How could you fail to tell me, Laird? I am your mother! Must I hear such important news from *her*—despicable Lady Henceforth?"

"I am sure I don't know what you mean." Laird's startled gaze sought out Anne.

Anne shook her head, ever so slightly, hoping he took her meaning that she and his mother had not discussed the real reason she had entered Laird's bedchamber that fateful night.

"My son is a *hero*, and a bashful hero, it seems,

for he did not even think to tell his own mother."
Lady MacLaren wrung her hands. "Everyone
must know. Oh, they will in St. Albans soon
enough. I have seen to that. But, la, we must
return to London—*unless* . . . No, I have a better idea!" She turned and without a thought to
Anne and Laird, stalked from the library.

Laird dropped back into his seat and rested
his head in his hand. "I am a hero now?"

Anne scurried over to the desk and leaned
over it toward him. "Well, yes, it seems so. And
Laird, you were ever so brave."

"Tell me, Anne, how has our predicament
worsened so much in the span of a day?"

Anne slapped her hand upon the polished
desktop in excitement. "Actually, it has gotten
better! I have made great strides in redeeming
you."

"Breaking Lady Henceforth's nose strengthens
our position?" he said, lifting his head to look at
her. There was no way this was possible. "Tell
me one thing, Anne. Breaking her nose with the
door of my carriage *was* an accident, wasn't it?"

"Oh, absolutely. A complete accident. I didn't
even know whose nose I'd broken until your

mother addressed her as Lady Henceforth in the apothecary shop."

"Thank God for small blessings." Even he could hear suppressed laughter edging his words. He turned more fully in his chair and absently rested his large hand over her slender fingers. "So tell me how we benefit from her broken nose."

"Because she likes me. She believes somehow that, through our association with you, we are kindred souls." Anne's eyes brightened, and she waited as he tried to decipher her meaning.

"I am sorry, Anne, but I do not know what you mean."

"She told me that she could not marry you once she learned of your behavior in London. She shared more sordid details than I cared to hear, that is for certain."

"Anne, I told you why she cried off." Laird felt a twinge of worry. It bothered him somehow that Anne could come to think of him as the rotten rogue he had been, rather than the man he was today.

"She asked why I would marry a man with such a black reputation."

Suddenly Laird understood. "And you told her I was no longer that man."

"Yes, I did." Anne lifted her chin proudly.

"You beauty!" Laird leapt from his chair, grabbed Anne's face between his palms, pulled her against him, and kissed her fully on the lips. The moment he'd done it, he knew it was wrong. Impulsive.

But Anne didn't resist. Instead she sighed suddenly, and to his surprise, he felt her body soften gently against his. Her unexpected response made him astonishingly hard.

Laird hadn't anticipated the carnal stirrings and released her at once, fumbling unsuccessfully for a reasonable explanation. "I apologize, Anne. I-I didn't mean . . . I shouldn't have." He met her gaze. "I-I was only so happy that you were able to talk to her."

"Oh, I know. No need for any sort of apology." As if she was confused by her own response to his kiss, Anne's eyebrows migrated toward her nose. "I was . . . happy, too." She took an unsteady step backward. Then a grin appeared upon her lips. "Though you do realize that while you claim that you are no longer the heartless man you once were, you do still have a definite rakish streak."

"'Tis true; it is part of who I am." He crossed

his hands over his heart. "But this rake has a heart and a conscience." He cast his eyes piously downward.

"Yes, you do, which is fortunate, because it is very important that we remain honest with each other if we are going to convince the world that we are happily engaged." The tone of her words was unusual, almost a warning.

"I agree." There was an underlying meaning to her words. Laird knew this, though he could not discern what it might be.

Anne looked him over for a long minute, allowing her gaze to linger upon his eyes as if she looked for something there. Then she smiled, as if pleased by what she saw. "But I know you already know this."

Laird paused. The tone of her statement sounded more like a question. "You needn't worry, Anne, I agree completely. It is imperative that we both be forthcoming with each other." He met her smile with his own. "But I know *you* already know this as well."

Anne laughed richly, tempting Laird's smile to broaden. When her smile dissolved, she tapped a finger to her lower lip. Thrice she started to say something more, but stopped short of speaking.

Oh no. "You might as well say whatever you must, Anne." Laird squinted his eyes and bared his teeth as if preparing for the worst.

Anne chuckled beneath her breath. "Um . . . since we are being forthcoming, I really ought to tell you the story of how we met . . . before your mother returns."

Laird groaned. "That bad, is it?"

Chapter 11

How to Tell a Fantastic Tale

MacLaren Hall
One week later

The ring of distinguished guests surrounding the dance floor heaved and contracted as more ladies and gentlemen, many from as far away as London, funneled into MacLaren Hall.

Laird bent at his knees, careful not to crease his ivory and gold-shot waistcoat, so that Lady MacLaren might hear him over the din of the crowd. "Mother, did you invite everyone who might have ever heard of our family to the betrothal ball?"

"It would seem that way, would it not?" Lady MacLaren chuckled merrily. "Oh, do not be cross with me. I wanted everyone of consequence to learn of my newly engaged son's heroic deed . . . and to meet his lovely betrothed, Anne."

"But, Mother, the heroic deed never—"

"Ah, here she comes now." The countess elbowed Laird in his side. "Isn't she lovely this eve? Sir Lumley had the gown sent directly from London especially for the occasion. Generous one, that gentleman." Lady MacLaren smiled brightly as Anne approached them at the perimeter of the floor. "Oh, your gown is perfect, dear."

Anne smiled meekly and dropped the countess a curtsy.

Laird's breath hitched in his throat as Anne drew alongside him and accepted his belatedly proffered arm.

Her gold satin gown reflected the candlelight shining down from the crystal chandeliers, making her shimmer and glow like the sun itself.

"You are lovely this evening, Anne," Laird told her without hesitation.

She glanced up at him through her thick lashes, meeting his appreciative gaze with her astonishing golden eyes. "Thank you, Lord MacLaren. You are looking quite *heroic* yourself."

Laird nodded politely. He had convinced himself that he wore the midnight-blue cutaway coat and ivory waistcoat so that he might look his best in the event Lady Henceforth attended, despite her injury. Now, after hearing Anne's generous comment about his appearance, he knew he had been fooling himself. He had wanted to look his best for Anne.

Lady MacLaren stood on her toes surveying the ocean of guests, then, as if she'd spotted land, leveled her hand at her brow. "Aha! There they are. The prattle mouths I've been waiting for: Lady Kentchurch and Mrs. Devonport. Remain here, son. I will bring them to you and Miss Anne. They must meet you both."

"Oh, jolly good." Laird turned and looked down at Anne standing at his side.

He could see in her face, her stance, her sudden stillness, that she was utterly petrified. Her golden eyes were wide and blank, and her delicately tinted lips—no doubt the handiwork of Solange, the lady's maid's—was fixed in a perpetual rose-hued smile, the sort one usually sees on dolls.

"Don't worry, lass. The crowd is large and the room so filled with noise that you need do nothing but smile. And it seems you have mastered that quite well."

At his teasing, she broke her stunned gaze and playfully narrowed her eyes at him. "Promise me that you will not leave my side, Laird, and we shall manage admirably. You will see."

Lady MacLaren bustled forward with the two stout matrons in tow. "Just then, the horse reared up, flinging her over the railing. As she fell, she struck her head on the edge of the bridge, rendering her quite senseless, before she plunged straight into the Serpentine."

The two older ladies gasped and turned their gazes to Anne for confirmation. Anne nodded her head forlornly, then tucked her arm around Laird's and smiled adoringly up at him.

"My son, the Earl of MacLaren, leapt atop the bridge railing and dove in after the poor, drowning gel—and saved her life." Lady MacLaren sucked in a deep breath and slapped her hands to her chest. "He might have been killed himself, but his thoughts were only with rescuing the Miss Anne Royle, who is now his betrothed."

Mrs. Devonport's eyes welled with tears, and she dabbed their corners with a lacy handkerchief. "So romantic. Fate brought the two of you together." She sighed dreamily.

"You are a true hero, Lord MacLaren," Lady Kentchurch added. "Why did I not know of this? Surely one would think that the *Times*, at least, would have reported such a heroic deed."

Anne drew a staggered breath, and the muscles of Laird's back tightened. What story would she concoct this time?

"You are correct, Lady Kentchurch. But unfortunately the newspapers could not report the details, because no one knew the identities of the drowning woman and her hero," Anne said. "Once Lord MacLaren urged the water from my lungs and I was breathing again, he brought me immediately to my family in Berkeley Square. Of course, he sought not thanks nor reward for his act of heroism. Instead, being the good gentleman he is, he called the next day to ascertain that I had recovered. Then he called the next day, too. And the next. And now . . . we are *betrothed*!"

Laird looked upon Anne in amazement. How could she possibly claim shyness as a fault? There was nothing the least bit reserved about the spitfire. Vivacious, imaginative, and entertaining were the words he would use to describe her. She was a complete delight.

But, sadly, a horrible liar.

Laird chuckled to himself. With each retelling, Anne's story seemed to grow grander.

Anne felt Laird gently draw her closer to his side. "My dear ladies," he said to the countess and the two "prattle mouths," "would you please excuse us. I promised to introduce Anne to our neighbors the Middletons, and I just spied them entering."

The three older women bobbed their heads as Laird whisked Anne from their fold and led her toward the outer band of guests.

"The Middletons?" Anne asked, turning to look up at Laird. "Your mother introduced me to the family. You were there." She looked quizzically at him.

"Did she? I must have forgotten." Laird glanced down at her and grinned. "Well, so much the better. I shan't have to track the pair down in this melee of satin and lace. Mayhap we should concentrate on locating the refreshment table instead. What say you, *darling*?"

"I agree. I must admit, recounting your heroics

has already left my lips quite parched." Anne's step lightened as Laird wrapped his arm around her like a shawl, holding her close as he wove a pathway toward the doors.

"No doubt." His dark eyebrow flicked upward as they entered the passage and neared the long tables topped with trays of sugary morsels and savories.

Two footmen ladled arrack punch into waiting cups, while others filled glistening goblets with lemonade.

Laird snatched two goblets from the tray of a footman heading for the ballroom and handed one to Anne. "And might I say, the touch about my being too noble to seek credit for my deed . . . inspired."

"Why, thank you, Lord MacLaren." Anne barely had finished her words before Laird turned and plucked a strawberry from a bowl on the table and rolled it across her lower lip. "Care for something sweet?"

She met his gaze and nodded her head slowly. She opened her mouth and allowed Laird to hold its tip just inside. She bit into the berry, allowing the sweet juice to spread over her tongue before closing her mouth upon the fruit.

Laird raised the remaining half of the berry and sucked it through his lips into the warmth of his mouth, then licked the tip of his thumb and finger with his tongue. "Sweet. But not half so delicious as you, Anne."

She knew what he was doing. He played a lovers' game, transforming the simplest gesture into seduction. But when she played along, she meant it.

Anne searched Laird's eyes, peering deep, wondering if he felt something for her . . . or if he only engaged in some rakish amusement. She did not relent in her gaze. She had to know, and if she just looked hard enough, long enough, she would see his heart revealed on his face.

A muscle near his jaw twitched and Laird flinched, as if unnerved by the intensity of her probing gaze.

Anne tore her unsettling gaze from him and redirected it to the punch glistening inside her goblet. She was about to drink when a loud voice broke free of the chatter filling the passage, drawing the attention of nearly everyone partaking of refreshment.

"The second set is about to begin!"

Anne turned to see a woman gesturing to a

gentleman standing beside Laird. The heavyset man tipped back his head and drained his goblet. "God, I hate dancing," he grumbled, but still he obediently headed for the ballroom doorway. The woman snatched his arm and relentlessly dragged him toward the dance floor.

"Second set." Laird gestured for Anne to sip from her goblet, then he lifted it away and set the glasses on the table. "Shall we, Anne?"

Excitedly she looped her arm around his.

Inside Anne, a bloom of hope unfolded, coaxed forth by the warmth of his smile. Could it be that Laird felt, at least in small part, as she did? That their relationship was more than a ruse—that it was becoming something deeper—*something real*?

Laird led her straight to the center of the floor, urging other dancers to make room for them in the heart of the column.

Other women in her line leaned forward and turned their heads to peek at Anne. As the dancers waited for the music to begin, Anne could hear bits of the other women's whispers about her. They all seemed to wish to know her, Anne Royle, the woman who had tamed the rakish Lord MacLaren. The gel from Cornwall who had claimed his heart.

Prickly heat rose up from beneath her bodice and colored her décolletage, her throat, and her cheeks. The attention was nearly overwhelming to her senses, but Anne held her head high. She lifted her eyes to gaze at Laird, and found him already looking at her. His back was straight and his shoulders broad and elegant. He looked to each side, silently addressing the other dancers, tipping his head to Anne between each acknowledgment.

Anne bashfully looked down at her slippers. It was as though Laird was proudly indicating to the other gentlemen that she belonged to him.

She raised her eyes and met Laird's gaze as the music began. Anne reached out her right hand and clasped Laird's as they and another couple crossed the column of dancers. Then they joined their left hands as they circled back to their start positions. Their gazes never wavered.

With a firm, possessive grasp, Laird cupped her fingers in his, and together they chasséd to the center and back again, before casting to second place.

Anne felt breathless, though hardly from exertion. She'd danced this very step dozens of times before, but this time she was acutely aware of her handsome partner. The heat from his hand, from his body near hers, seemed to trail down her arm like a caress.

He placed his other hand at the small of her back, and Anne nearly gasped from the sensation. He touched her precisely in the way that every other gentleman dancer did when guiding his partner, she knew that. But somehow, the gentle pressure of Laird's warm fingers moving slightly over her body felt far more intimate.

Made her think of things a maiden should not consider.

And yet she did.

Thoughts of him plagued her mind nearly every minute of every day—since the moment he found her in his bedchamber ... and kissed her. What was it about this man that intrigued her so?

Anne abandoned the hopeless question. It really didn't matter. It was a cruel fact that her time with Laird would end on the last day of the season, if not before.

Whether her heart wished it or not.

From Laird's height and angle, the candle-light from the sparkling chandeliers above cast a magical golden aura around Anne. Perhaps it was a trick of the eye, but the glow from the tapers' flames did not seem to flatter anyone else so much as it did his betrothed.

His betrothed. Not his false fiancée. Not his partner in this scheme.

Sod it. For a moment, he had fooled himself into believing their concocted story—that they were betrothed and would soon be wed.

Anne turned her delicate porcelain face toward him and smiled serenely. Her eyes were alight with happiness, and she laughed as they grasped right hands overhead and she crossed the set allemande and returned again.

The sound of her laughter made him laugh as well, but it also made him consider her in a way he consciously hadn't before.

Anne appealed to his every sense in a way he could not describe. Could not even begin to explain. All he knew was that no other woman in the ballroom, no woman he had ever met, possessed an allure to match hers.

Certainly he had chanced upon greater beauties. More clever conversationalists. Quicker wits. Only he could not recall a single woman who drew him like Anne. There never had been a woman who made him yearn to be with her, every moment of every day . . . and night. Made him realize that, until she stole into his life, he had not truly been living—he'd simply been existing. Passing the days, the weeks, the years.

What was it about her that made her so irresistible to him?

A fullness expanded inside his chest as he realized what he had been denying. He was beginning to feel things for her that he'd never allowed himself to feel for anyone before.

She was chipping away at the stone that had hardened around his heart.

She was making him *feel*.

He was happy when he was with Anne, this beautiful, unique, young woman from the depths of Cornwall.

He laughed softly to himself. *Gorblimey*. Who would have ever guessed it? Perhaps for the first time in his life, he was truly happy.

And the reason was Miss Anne Royle.

He needed to tell her. He had no idea what he would say, or even how she would respond. All he knew was that she had changed his life, somehow, and he had to let her know. Had to tell her how she made him feel.

Tonight.

* * *

The last of the guests left the ball by four of the clock, allowing Lady MacLaren and her staff to totter off to their beds.

Laird and Apsley were sharing a final draught of brandy in the library.

"A bloody hero. Fancy that." Apsley grinned. "Do you think I could borrow your Anne to boost up my reputation tomorrow? Lord knows I could use a few heroic deeds to keep my family out of my private life."

"I do apologize, Apsley, but I only *boost* the reputation of my fiancé."

Laird and Apsley swung their heads around to see Anne standing in the doorway.

She walked across the library and joined the two gentlemen near the desk. "And, since I can only be promised to one gentleman at a time . . ." She fashioned a look forlorn of all hope. "Well, you understand, don't you, Apsley?"

"Anne, I thought you were abed." As soon as the words left Laird's mouth, the image of Anne in his own bed, her pale skin bared to his touch, filled his mind.

Hoping to whisk the heady notion from his mind, he busied himself by filling a glass with wine punch and handing it to her.

"Oh, I shouldn't. I have had two glasses already—and you know how wine affects me." She tossed a covert wink at him as she brought the crystal to her mouth and sipped from it anyway.

He watched how her body curved as she tilted the glass, and he imagined it curving against him. Then he felt his bollocks tighten with excitement, and he knew he was lost.

"I was looking for something to read—again. I wrote a note to my sister Elizabeth asking her to send down a few books if she could spare them. Haven't received any *letters* in reply, however." She touched the glass to her lips and drank deeply of the wine punch, then turned her delicately boned countenance to face him directly. The tip of her pink tongue slipped across her lower lip. "You were going to assist me with *my* search of the library, Lord MacLaren."

Ah, the letters. Laird stepped behind the desk to conceal the growing evidence of his misplaced desire for her. "Yes, I did promise."

"Did you find anything yet that might interest me?" Anne raised her blond eyebrows questioningly, but her gaze lingered upon his chest.

"Not yet, but I have not given up."

Then it occurred to Apsley just what their veiled

conversation was all about. "Damn me!" He started to laugh, coughing on his last swig of brandy. He waved his lace-fringed hand in the air. "You are both searching for those bloody letters—in *here*!"

"Shh!" Anne angled a vertical finger to her lips, drawing Laird's attention to them and holding it there. Making him want to taste them. To kiss them.

"Oh, do let me help with the search." Apsley's eyes flashed excitedly as looked back and forth between Laird and Anne. "This will be such fun."

"Splendid idea, Apsley." Laird clapped his friend between his shoulder blades.

"What?" Anne furrowed her graceful winged eyebrows. "He can't—"

"Search the stables?" Laird broke in. "No, I don't suppose he could, even if it is the only place we have not searched."

Apsley laughed. "I see what you are up to here. Think it would be great fun to watch the viscount dig around in the muck, don't you?"

"Well, you asked. And the stables have not been searched." Laird lifted the decanter of brandy to Apsley, who shook his head.

"No, no. I am off. Being the third carriage

wheel has never been my preference—unless the other two are buxom redheads. In that case, I might be swayed." Apsley chuckled to himself as he sauntered off for the doorway, but turned before stepping into the passage. "But I will take on the stables at first light . . . or . . . certainly before noon. Only, hear me now, if *I* find the letters, I get to read every one of them—first. Good night, all."

"The stables?" Anne brought her bare hand to her mouth and laughed richly.

Laird's lips twitched. "My father would have never entered such an untidy place. Apsley can search as long as he likes."

Anne swallowed the last of her cordial, then circled around the desk to where Laird stood. She raised her empty glass to him.

"You are not asking for more, are you? What about your delicate constitution?"

"Oh stop, Laird. You know very well that I was not truly looking for an unoccupied chamber pot when I came into your bedchamber." She raised her glass and allowed him to fill it.

"I know, *darling*. You were looking for *me*."

Anne smiled almost coquettishly as she set her glass upon the desk. She grabbed his shoulders playfully and yanked him to her. "How did you know, *my dear*?" She tilted back her head and made to laugh at their joke, but she didn't. Their eyes met, and both became instantly silent.

He looked at her, wondering who would be the first to put an end to this dangerous, teasing game. In the end, he decided it would be he. He cupped his hand behind her neck and pulled her into a rough kiss.

Anne leaned back, but did not leave his embrace. "Why do you do this, Laird?" She shook her head so slowly and moved so slightly that at first he didn't comprehend her question. "Why do you play the rake whenever I come too close? When a moment becomes weighted?"

Laird averted his gaze and sighed. "I-I honestly don't know." He peered into her eyes again and waited, knowing somehow that she would offer some answer.

"I think you do. I think it is your armor. Your protection against intimacy."

Laird forced a hard laugh. "Kissing you is my protection against intimacy?"

"Kissing me, like that, is no different than pushing me away. Keeping any chance of tenderness at a distance."

She touched his cheek with her fingertips. "But it doesn't have to be that way. You are a strong man, a kind man, a noble man—a man capable of anything you set your heart and mind to do. Laird, you don't have to pretend you don't care, when you do."

Laird turned his head away, but Anne caught his jaw with her hand and made him face her again. "You do not have to protect yourself from me. I'll never hurt you."

Something broke inside him then, and he wanted nothing more than to hold Anne to him. To kiss her. To love her. His eyes burned as he stared at her face.

Christ above, she is so beautiful.

Instinctively Laird brought his hands to her waist and pulled her firmly against him. He wanted to tell her that it wasn't the cad that drove him to her now. It was his need for her. But words failed him.

At his touch, Anne stiffened, and an expression of circumspection came over her.

How he ached for her, and he knew with certainty that she could feel his hardness against her now. He readied himself for the sting of a slap to his cheek.

But it did not come.

Instead her breath came fast and hot, and still she did not pull away. Her gaze, filled with wary expressions of arousal and alarm, lingered on his mouth. "We're engaged," she said. "I do not think the world would think anything of it if we simply kissed."

Rather than give her another moment to reconsider her position, he angled his head to kiss her. Laird pressed his lips to hers, and held them to his, sucking gently, then sliding his tongue along her lower lip.

"Oh, *my Laird*," she murmured, the moment he lifted his mouth.

Laird smiled at her. "That's right, lass. You've got the right of it now." His voice was deep and husky, almost a growl, and it tickled her ear, and lower, too.

She felt the roughness of skin against her chin, the taste of the brandy on his lips, and all she knew was that she did not want this bliss to end.

Her resolve to remain impassive had all but dissolved. She wanted to go on pretending she really was his. Wanted to continue imagining a future with Laird . . . as his wife.

She wanted more than a kiss.

Her nipples hardened beneath the smooth satin of her gown, and she knew he became instantly aware of this, deepening her disgrace.

She felt a tug on the ribbon at the scoop of her neckline, and the tips of her breasts, peeking out from her silken chemise, were bared to him. A flush swept up from her middle, blossoming on Anne's cheeks.

His hands tightened around her waist, whisking her around, and sitting her on the desk. He took her mouth again and kissed it, hard and deep, while pushing her knees apart, and moving between them.

Only a wisp of a chemise and a cool sheath of satin separated her core from his maleness. The thought drove her mad.

He leaned against her, and she slammed her hands behind her on the desk to keep from falling flat onto her back.

Laird slid a hand against her back, then dipped his head, and with his mouth, nudged one of her nipples free, and then the full roundness of her breast followed. His free hand cupped it, and he raised its pink peak to his mouth, drawing color into her nipple as he licked and sucked.

Anne moaned. This was so wrong, she knew, but nothing had ever felt so right to her as this moment. A shiver fluttered through her body, making her breast quiver.

His gentle hand slid inside her chemise and freed her other breast, and now he stroked her swells, flicking thumbs over the hardened tips.

Anne squirmed, and she flung up one hand, cupped it behind his neck, and drew his mouth to her breast once more, urging him to loose his magic on her, to bring her nipples, each in turn, into the furnace of his mouth.

A tension began to wind in her core as he fed on her, and intuitively she wound her legs around his muscled thighs and pulled herself against him.

Laird moaned, sending unbearably sweet vibrations through her nipple. He leaned up and plunged his tongue into her mouth, sliding inside along the soft flesh.

Lifting her other hand from the desk, she grabbed his shoulder and fell onto her back, pulling him down atop her.

She felt his hand, pinned beneath her, pull free, and then she felt it slide up her leg, burrowing under her skirt and chemise, riding up past the ribbon that held her stocking. Then his fingers trailed up the smooth, sensitive skin of her inner thigh. And he touched her.

There.

His fingers moved between her folds, stroking her, drawing forth the slickness of her woman-hood.

"Laird," she gasped.

He stopped then.

No, no, don't stop.

He lurched back and stared down at her thighs spread open to him.

At her face.

He backed up and pulled her skirts down over her knees. "I-I'm sorry, Anne. Bloody hell, I haven't changed." Disgust was plain in his voice. "I haven't."

He stared at her as he stalked around the desk and out of the library, leaving a trail of oaths in the air behind him.

Anne crawled from the desk and folded onto the floor. "God, I am such a fool."

Chapter 12

How to Find Your Way in the Dark

The chamber lamp Anne carried cast a perfectly round glow on the treads as her leaden legs plodded up the grand staircase and down the long passage.

She'd walked this same path dozens of times, in the day as well as the night, but never before had she felt so lost and in need of a guiding light.

There was a glowing coal fire in the fireplace, and the ewer had been filled with hot water and set upon a small brass brazier before the hearth to preserve its warmth.

She poured the water into the basin on the washstand, stripped off every thread of clothing, and scrubbed a dampened cloth roughly against her skin. Bah! As if it were possible to wash away her humiliation so that her dignity might return.

It wasn't his fault, not truly. She had allowed herself to give in to the fantasy they had constructed together.

She had let herself believe that this farce was somehow becoming real.

She had given in to the heated, passionate longings that burgeoned inside her for him.

At least she hadn't fallen in love.

She was such a fool. Laird had reacted exactly as she should have expected him to. He told her he was a rake at heart, and part of him always would be. He responded to her sensual game, matched her lustfulness. However, just when the blackguard he claimed he used to be would have slaked his need with her, Laird had simply turned away.

He spared her ruin.

For the second time.

Dear God. Laird *had* changed.

By the horrified look on his face before he raced from the library, she was certain he believed himself wicked beyond redemption.

The wine she'd consumed was making her confused and weary. So Anne quickly dried herself, then slipped her dressing gown over her shoulders and set about pulling the pins from her hair.

But her comb, however, was nowhere in sight. A maid had likely put it away. Anne pulled the top handle of the low bedside chest of drawers, but the flickering candlelight did not reach the depths of the drawer. Anne fumbled her hand around inside for the comb, when suddenly she felt a folded sheet of foolscap wedged far back, ready to fall out of reach.

Heavens, could this be one of the letters?

Her heart pounded madly as she dropped to her knees and shoved her arm deep behind the drawer, and after a long minute, withdrew the letter. But there was just this one. Still, it could be . . .

She held it near the chamber lamp and, with shaking hands, opened the letter from its folds. It was written to Laird. Her gaze dropped to the signature, and her excitement with it: Graham.

Blast. Just one more disappointment.

With a sigh, Anne slowly refolded the letter and set it down on the chest of drawers. She leaned over and blew out the candle, then curled up on the edge of the tester bed and closed her eyes.

What happened in the library wasn't Laird's fault.

He had changed.

He was a gentleman.

She'd be sure to tell him so in the morning.

It was still dark when Anne was jolted from her sleep. The sound of carriage wheels spraying pebbles against the front of the house propelled her from the tester bed and to the window.

She peered down just as a footman raised a lantern and opened the carriage door. Wild, drunken female laughter burst from inside the cab.

Anne pressed her hands and forehead against the cool windowpane, hoping for a better look at the occupants in the carriage.

Apsley climbed down the step to the gravel with what appeared to be an empty bottle in his hand. A woman's bare arm reached out and caught his sleeve and tried to pull him inside again. Apsley laughed and dropped the bottle on the ground, and then he obliged her.

And then, she saw *him*.

Laird stepped down unsteadily from the carriage. His foot slipped from the step, and he came down hard on the gravel.

He braced himself with a groping hand against the door. He looked back inside the cab, just before a sable-haired miss leaned her head outside the cab and angled her mouth toward him for a kiss.

Anne's body quaked and she lurched back from the window.

Why? Why? Oh God, she could watch no more. It hurt too much.

She whisked the brown velvet curtains closed against the offending sight. Her eyes welled with hot tears as she turned and ran for her bed. Great sobs rose up inside her throat. She tore the sheets and coverlets back this time, then climbed into bed and threw them over her head to block out the sound, too.

What had she expected?

Perhaps Lady Henceforth was right all along. A tiger cannot change its stripes.

Laird was and always would be a rake. He hadn't changed.

Anne had just been too dim-witted to realize it.

Chapter 13

How to Become a Hero

"**N**eedles and pins!" Anne sat up in the tester bed and scowled at the chirping blue bird outside her window that had had the cheerful audacity to wake her.

She flipped onto her stomach and scrunched a pillow around her head to block out the bird's happy song. But it was no use. She could still hear it.

It was just as well, she ultimately decided. She rolled onto her back and grudgingly sat up. She should dress and depart the house as soon as possible, after all, if she wanted to avoid Laird in the breakfast room.

Lord above. There was no way she could face him today. Not after what happened last night.

But he wouldn't be in her life much longer.

Not if she could help it. Anne flicked her hair behind her shoulders. She would not be angry with him, because he was what he was. *She* was the goose last eve to have convinced herself that he truly had changed.

But she had promised Laird to make Lady Henceforth see the gentleman in him, and in doing so earn her own freedom to cry off. So that was what she would do in earnest . . . beginning this very morn.

Anne did not break her fast, or even enter the breakfast room. With her black luck, Laird and Apsley wouldn't have gone to bed yet, and would be sitting at the table munching on toasted bread with butter or sipping steaming cups of tea.

Anne's stomach growled at the thought of a bite to eat, but instead of chancing a glance into the room, she gathered up her shawl and satin-banded straw hat and headed out the door.

The blue bird had called it right. It was a lovely morning—a welcome change after the horridness of last night. Just the sort of day to sweeten her sour mood.

As she walked into the drive, she stumbled over Apsley's empty bottle. Angrily she snatched it up and flung it as far as she could. When she heard it shatter, she smiled and began her walk again.

The air was soft and already beginning to warm in the heat of the sun. The sky was cloudless, as vibrant a blue as Laird's eyes.

Good Lord, where did that thought come from?

His rakish blue eyes, she amended. *Remember that.*

Anne hastened her pace, trying her best to think happy thoughts—after all, she would soon be rid of Laird forever. That was reason enough for cheeriness, was it not?

She forced herself to smile. Yes, all in all, it was the perfect sort of day for a walk across the fields to Chasten Cottage, Lady Henceforth's charming stone . . . Well, to speak plainly, it was actually a manor house. Nothing less.

Anne wasn't sure why anyone would call the house a cottage, for it certainly wasn't. The house was quite huge by any standard. After all, what sort of cottage had a ballroom—even a modest one? Or a massive dining room fit for a visit from Queen Charlotte?

No, the only thing humble about Chasten Cottage, Anne decided, was its absurdly inappropriate name.

Anne lifted her hem higher and higher as she walked through the tall, cool grass. The sun had yet to burn the dew from the tips of the green stalks, and soon her stockings were sodden.

Blast. Perdition.

But still she trudged on, lifting a false smile to her lips again.

She had promised to convince Lady Henceforth that Lord MacLaren had changed—that he had become a gentleman. And that she would do—as quickly as possible. Maybe even this morn.

Yes, today would be the day that she fulfilled her bargain with the blue-eyed devil and could then return to London . . . and put that desk in the library out of her mind forever. Nothing good ever happened when she was near that desk.

She had searched most every room in MacLaren Hall already, and the letters had not been found. What if there never were any letters? Anne picked up her pace as she thought about this possibility.

The Old Rakes had tricked her sister into marrying the Duke of Blackstone—what if the old matchmakers had the same idea for her and Lord MacLaren? He was an earl, and a rake, which would make him just the sort of man they would choose.

No, preposterous. No, no, no. Even they would not go to these extremes to orchestrate such a match.

"Anne!"

She wrenched her head around. A horseman approached from the direction of MacLaren Hall.

"Anne, please wait."

Drat it all. Laird.

Chasten Cottage was not so far away. It couldn't be. She squinted at the rise beyond. It wasn't visible yet, but Lady MacLaren had mentioned that Lady Henceforth's property abutted the MacLaren north field, so it had to be close.

And so, Anne began to run.

"Anne, stop!" The sound of hoofbeats grew louder behind her, but she dared not look back at Laird.

After the rise ahead of her, the ground seemed to drop off downward, and beyond she could just make out a stream with a few flat stepping stones interspersed in the form of a make-do bridge. She made for that.

Laird had to be only a few yards behind her now. His call was insistent, but she wasn't going to stop for him.

"Anne—you've got to stop! Ahead of you—"

Anne's leading foot suddenly stepped into naught but air above a rocky crevasse. She tried to stop, but her momentum carried her forward, and she screamed as she slipped over the edge.

"Anne!" Laird leapt from his horse and ran to the precipice.

She dangled precariously, about two feet below the lip of the rock face, from a thick root poking between a crevice in the wall. Her golden eyes peered pleadingly up at him. She gasped, "Help me! *Please.*"

"Hold tight, Anne." Laird dropped to his chest and moved to the edge of the cliff. He reached down and grabbed her wrist. "I've got you. Now put your boots against the rock to get a foothold while I pull you up."

Anne nodded, and indeed scrambled up the wall as he lifted, until he was able to pull her over the lip to solid ground.

Laird had just rolled onto his back, pulling the

minx next to him, lest she try to run and get herself into an even worse predicament.

"Are you all right?" He felt the movement of her head nodding against his chest as she struggled to catch her breath.

"I-I scraped my knee," she panted. "Nothing more."

"Well done!" came a woman's familiar voice from the distance, followed by a rousing round of applause.

Laird sat up, and Anne along with him.

There on the far side of the crevasse, just up a tree-dotted hillock, stood four women of varied ages, shapes, and sizes. Easels and painting tables were set up behind them.

One of the women broke from the group and walked down the hill.

"It seems being a hero has become a way of life, my lord."

She started to laugh, but she stopped abruptly and patted the white plaster stretched across the bridge of her nose.

"*Constance*," Laird murmured.

"I told you, I can walk. Why, I could dance if I wished it!" Anne protested. "Put me down,

Laird, at once! Go see to your horse or something."

Laird carried her through the door of Mac-Laren Hall and into the drawing room, where he stretched her out upon a claret-hued damask settee. "I shall fetch Lady MacLaren's personal physician to make certain you are well."

"Not Doctor Willet, please." Anne settled her head in her hands. "After he plastered Lady Henceforth's nose, I am sure he already thinks me a menace to the whole of St. Albans."

"I shall send my mother to wait with you. Do not move." Laird raced from the room.

La, why was he making such a to-do about this? She flung her head back against the settee in frustration. He was probably just feeling guilty about last eve. Humiliating her, then heading off into the night with Apsley and his giggling barmaids.

That had to be why he was making such a fuss over her leg. After all, she had told him she was fine. Anne glanced down at her knee and winced. She was fine. She was . . . mostly.

Lady MacLaren hurried into the drawing room. At once her gaze targeted Anne's bare bloodstained knee. "Dear me, what now?" She called frantically for a maid to bring her water and a cloth, and immediately set about dabbing the blood off Anne's knee.

"Please, Lady MacLaren, there is no need to bother yourself. 'Tis but a scratch."

Gravel crunched and popped outside. Anne glanced over the back of the settee and out the window. She could just see the rear of a landau as it drew up before the house.

There was a knock at the door, and soon Lady Henceforth, a freckle-faced girl of perhaps fourteen summers, and two matrons were ushered into the drawing room.

Lady MacLaren came to her feet as Anne pulled herself upright on the settee. Her knee stung as she covered it once more with her chemise and Indian chintz walking gown. She forced a thin smile as Lady Henceforth introduced her aunts, Mrs. Forthwit and Mrs. Bean, and her young cousin, Hortense.

"We have to come to see to your welfare, Miss Royle." Lady Henceforth's words seemed genuinely filled with concern, but the almost amused expression in her eyes told Anne otherwise.

"And to meet the hero," Miss Hortense blurted, before she could be hushed.

"Well, the *hero* is not at home, but I am quite well." Anne smiled most hospitably, though her knee had really begun to throb.

"Yes, 'tis a scratch, that is all," Lady MacLaren quipped. "No need for anyone to be concerned. But thank you for coming." Her eyes narrowed as she met Lady Henceforth's gaze, but her smile remained hostess-worthy.

Anne knew it was difficult for Lady MacLaren to bear seeing the woman, who had so disgraced the family, now standing in the MacLaren drawing room. Anne had to commend her for her fortitude. Lady MacLaren's manners were impeccable. Truth to tell, Anne doubted she would be able to remain so calm were she in the same circumstance.

When it became clear that the ladies were not ready to depart, Lady MacLaren invited the women to sit, and then sent for tea.

"Is it true, Miss Royle, that you had drowned in the Serpentine and that Lord MacLaren breathed life back into your body?" Mrs. Bean leaned forward as she awaited the answer.

"Well," Anne sputtered, "in a manner of speaking, yes, he did."

The two aunts exchanged glances and tittered excitedly.

"He is such a strong and capable gentleman." Mrs. Forthwit addressed Lady MacLaren. "Of course you were not there, but less than an hour past we saw your son pluck Miss Royle from the face of a cliff and lift her into his arms as if she were as light as a bird."

"Good heavens, Anne!" Lady MacLaren's white eyebrows fluttered like dove's wings. "Laird did not mention a word of this to me. Only that you fell and injured your knee. Is this true, Anne?"

"Well, yes," Anne repeated. "More or less."

Lady MacLaren slapped her hands to her cheeks. "Do you mean you fell into the crevasse bordering the north fields?"

"Yes, yes, she did. We all saw her fall. We were painting just on the other side. If Lord MacLaren had not been there to save her, she would surely have fallen to her death!" Mrs. Bean exclaimed.

Anne brought a hand to her brow to conceal her rolling eyes. *Yes, but I wouldn't have fallen at all if he hadn't been chasing me.*

"Anne, you might have been killed." Lady MacLaren set her hand down upon Anne's knee. Anne gasped, and the older woman snatched back her hand. "I do apologize, daughter."

Daughter? Anne's heart thumped within her breast.

"Daughter?" Lady Henceforth flicked a sable eyebrow at the reference. "But Lord MacLaren and Miss Royle are only betrothed. A betrothal is but an ephemeral promise of something that has not yet come to be."

Poppy-colored blooms burst upon Lady Mac-Laren's cheeks. "Some people hold promises dearer than do others."

"What are you saying, Lady MacLaren?" Lady Henceforth goaded. "That I did not keep my promise to your son?"

Anne clenched her fist. Lady Henceforth was drawing dreadfully close to the edge of Anne's patience. It did not matter how much Laird had hurt her last eve, Anne was not about to allow Lady Henceforth to malign him—or hurt Lady MacLaren more than she had already.

The countess was too much of a lady to respond to Lady Henceforth, but her hands shook as she poured tea for them and their guests.

Lady Henceforth was not so gracious. "How could I honor a promise when *he*—"

"Saved a woman and her three . . . cats from a burning bakery in Cheapside the very day he

215

returned to London!" Anne blurted. "Surely you read of the incident in the London newspapers."

Gads, where did that lie come from? It just seemed to leap unbidden from her mouth and straight into the drawing room.

Lady Henceforth chuckled. "Oh, really? He rescued a woman *and* her cats? Somehow I am finding this story of yours quite incredible, Miss Anne."

Anne prayed that her cheeks would not flush with color from the lie. The cats, well, that might have been a bit much. But Laird *had* saved her this very day, after all. She owed it to him to defend his name.

"My word, I remembering reading about that fire. At least a dozen people died," Mrs. Forthwit said. "I did not know it was Lord MacLaren who saved the baker's wife . . . and cats as well, you say?"

"My son is very courageous," Lady MacLaren chimed in. She looked to Anne and gave a firm nod, as if her comment somehow bolstered Anne's own outlandish story of Laird's heroism.

"Mama, when will Lord MacLaren return?" Hortense said softly, turning to Mrs. Bean. "I want to meet the hero *today!*"

"Well, you can well understand why I immediately agreed to our betrothal," Anne said, most matter-of-factly. "I did not know him until he returned to London after his mourning. But I never met a better man in all my life. He is the most courageous, generous—did you know he gave a goodly sum to the Royal Military Hospital in Chelsea?—kindest gentleman I have ever had the honor to know."

Oh no. She'd done it again! She'd made him a hero thrice over, and now a philanthropist, too.

A chorus of appreciative sighs filled the air.

Hesitantly she glanced at Lady MacLaren, thinking that she would detect Anne's untruths immediately. But Lady MacLaren was smiling. Her eyes welled with pride as she gazed at Anne.

She had gone too far. Why did she do it?

Anne swallowed deeply, hoping to knock back into her throat whatever lie was next making its way to her lips.

Anne loathed lying. She was terrible at telling lies, even small white lies meant to spare someone's feelings. Always had been.

So why couldn't she seem to stop lying now?

Chapter 14

How to Save a Cat

"**S**he'll be right as March rain within a week." Doctor Willet finished wrapping the bandage around Anne's knee, then tied it off.

Laird saw the exasperated glance the doctor gave Anne as she looked down to adjust her skirts over her leg.

Then Doctor Willet swiveled around and gazed at Lady MacLaren. "Though you might try to convince her stay in the house for another fortnight—for her own good."

"Thank you so much for tending our Anne, Dr. Willet." She walked with him into the passage, complaining about the stiffness in her shoulders just after a soaking rain.

Laird closed the drawing room door until it

remained but a finger's width open. "Anne, I know we have only a few moments before my mother returns, so please, just listen to me. I'm sorry for last night."

She tried to wave him away, but instead he came closer. Anne's golden eyes began to glisten. "Wh-what is it about me that you find so repugnant?" she asked him.

"What?" Laird shook his head in confusion and knelt down beside the settee.

"Yes, what exactly is it? I need to know."

"Anne, I adore everything about you. You are amusing and beautiful, brave and kind." He tried to reach out to her, but she leaned away, making her desire to avoid his touch very clear.

"There must be something about me that you detest." She folded her arms tightly about her.

"Why are you co convinced?" Laird expelled a breath. "Because I did not make love to you?"

"Yes! At first I thought it was because you had changed—and wished to save me ruin. Because you were a gentleman. *You had changed*." Her voice trembled with emotion.

"Don't you understand, Anne? I haven't changed. I've tried, damn it, I have. But it's no use. I am irredeemable—a blackguard to my core. My father was right about me."

"I saw the horror on your face when you pulled away from me. I knew then that you no longer believed your own transformation. You doubted yourself. I had to talk to you. I had to help you see that you were wrong." Anne wiped a tear from her cheek with the back of her hand and looked directly at him. "Laird, I tried to wait up for you last night . . . but the wine. I fell asleep—"

"Anne."

Her expression changed then, grew harder. "—only to be awakened by you, and Apsley . . . and your lady friends arriving at the house."

"Anne, you must listen to me—they were Apsley's friends, not mine. I assure you, nothing happened."

"But I saw—"

"What, Anne?"

Her nostrils flared and her breath grew rapid. She sniffed back her tears. "*N-nothing.*" She pushed up past him and limped to the door. "Do excuse me, please."

"Anne!" Laird came to his feet and reached out a hand to her, but Anne had already disappeared into the passage. "In the library, I didn't, because I . . . I—" He closed his mouth and let his hand fall to his side. "Because I love . . ." His words trailed out into the empty drawing room, until they were enveloped by silence.

Lady MacLaren walked in through the open door, teasing Laird for an instant with the thought that Anne had returned.

"Laird, why didn't tell me about the fire? You are truly a hero."

Laird straightened his back, willing away whatever remnants of visible emotion clung to him.

"Dear Anne is so proud; she could not seem to stop herself from telling everyone all about it."

"The fire?"

Lady MacLaren's eyes sparkled merrily, and her mouth puckered to suppress a chuckle. "Oh yes, a terrible fire—with cats."

"Oh dear God." Laird ran his hands through his hair. "Seriously, she said . . . cats?"

Lady MacLaren could withhold her mirth no longer, and laughter burst from her lips. "Oh yes. Cats. And you, my dear, are their hero."

Anne threw herself onto the bed and clapped her hands over her damp eyes. "Why can't I rein in my heart when he is near?" Balling her fist, she slammed it to the bedding.

Lord knew, she had tried so hard to remain calm and serene in Laird's presence, but from the moment he closed the drawing room door and looked at her with that sorrowful expression of his, she knew she should just limp away. But she hadn't, and an aching wound seemed to rip open within her chest, giving way to bleeding words and tearful accusations.

She was so pitiful.

She should have never come to St. Albans. Playing the role of fiancée to a rogue of the first sort was far more difficult than she ever imagined. She was far too inexperienced in the ways of ordinary gentlemen. Whatever made her think she could parry with a man as extraordinary as Laird? He was far too charming. Too clever. Too handsome. Too . . . skilled. Anne flushed hotly at the memory of his luscious mouth . . . his wandering fingers upon her—

"No, no, no!" She scrubbed her hands over her face. *Do not even think such thoughts!*

She flung herself upright and sat on the edge of the tester bed. All she needed was to stop deluding herself that Laird was interested in her as anything but a means to appear respectable—and remain focused on the completion of her two tasks: search for the hidden letters and help Lady Henceforth see the good in Laird. That's all.

Now that she was aware of her times of weakness with him, she could manage them. It would be simple enough. She would just remain stoic and phlegmatic whenever she found herself in the unfortunate position of being alone with him.

Simple.

An hour later, Laird spied Anne cutting flowers in the garden. Her face no longer appeared mottled, her eyes were not red, and her countenance was quite serene. Yes, he decided, it was time to try another apology.

As quietly as he could, he opened the French window and stepped onto the garden path.

"Anne."

She startled at his voice and began to hurry away, but she stilled abruptly. She turned slowly to him and raised her chin. "I was just thinking I could use a rake in the garden."

He supposed he deserved that. "Anne, I am sorry."

"No need to apologize. I am quite recovered now." Like the dragonfly circling a puddle alongside the garden path, Anne's gaze flitted lightly over him.

Ah, a direct approach was not going to reach Anne. Another way, perhaps.

Laird raised his palms and offered her a small smile. "Cats?"

For the briefest instant, he could almost swear that a smile flickered on her lips.

"Well, I didn't know if the woman I read about in the *Times* had children." Her throat muscles contracted as she swallowed. "Cats . . . just slipped off my tongue. I cannot explain it, so I shan't."

"So, please let me see if I have a full accounting of my heroics before I speak to my mother or anyone else in St. Albans again."

Anne nodded once.

"I rescued you from drowning. I pulled a woman and . . . her cats from a burning building, and it is my grandest desire to improve the welfare of humanity through charity. Oh, and I rescued you from certain death after you fell from a cliff. Do I have this right, Anne?"

Anne's eyes were wide as tea saucers when she nodded again.

"I haven't left anything out?"

"Not yet."

Laird stared at her in disbelief. "Yet?"

"I haven't been able to locate a London newspaper since we've arrived." Anne cringed. "I read the news and, lud, I do not know why, but somehow, of late, the stories emerge, transformed into heroic stories about *you*."

"Damn it all, Anne, these tales must stop."

Her eyes flashed. "Don't you think I am aware of that? But Lady Henceforth can just be so politely ... *awful*. Another few words and your mother would have been in tears. It was either stuff my handkerchief into Lady Henceforth's mouth—which would have been difficult given my bleeding knee—or say something that would have the same effect. I chose the latter."

Could Anne be speaking of his Lady Henceforth? Constance, the elegant, soft-spoken widow who desired nothing more than to read in her garden, to sing when the occasion presented, and to play the pianoforte? Surely not.

It struck him then. This was not about Lady Henceforth at all. This was about last night.

"What did she say to my mother that so upset her?"

"Oh, I do not recall . . . precisely." Anne waved him off. "She was about to attack your character. So I stopped her."

"By making me out to be some larger-than-life heroic figure?" Laird retorted sarcastically.

"*Yes*." Anne limped toward a crimson-budded rose bush. "Haven't we spoken enough today? I will not discuss anything more. Besides, this was all *your* idea."

"My idea?"

"Yes, yours completely. I did not wish to perpetuate the lie of our engagement. *You* forced me to continue this outrageous charade. *You* made me agree to help you redeem your character in the eyes of Lady Henceforth."

"And *this*, Anne, is what you think I meant?"

"I *told* you I could not do this. This was all far beyond my nature. And yet you pressed me." Anne limped toward the door and opened it. Before she stepped into the house, she looked over her shoulder at him. "So *this* is what you get—*cats*."

Damn it all. This day had gone straight to hell.

And all he had wanted to do this morning was to find Anne and tell her that he was sorry.

Two days later

Anne had found reasons, weak and dreadfully transparent though they were, to avoid being left alone with Laird for two full days.

Today, when she was afforded her first real excuse for leaving MacLaren Hall, Laird was nowhere to be seen. Anne gave a parting glance up at Laird's bedchamber window and then boarded the carriage Lady Henceforth had sent to bring her to Chasten Cottage for tea.

Oh, she doubted Lady Henceforth was just being kind to send transportation in consideration of her bandaged knee. Women like her always had an ulterior reason for gestures of kindness. More likely she didn't want to risk Laird coming to rescue Anne from some unforeseen accident.

Anne's head thumped back against the leather cushion as the driver snapped his whip and the carriage lurched forward.

She dreaded Lady Henceforth's invitation to tea but felt obliged to accept.

She had made a Laird a promise to redeem his reputation, and she would keep it, if only to hasten her own return to London. Anne stared blankly out the window as the carriage rolled down the pitted road.

Today she would take more care with her words. She gave her head a resolute nod. There would be no more talk of dangerous rescues . . . or cats.

Oh, she had made such a cake of herself.

Cats. What had she been thinking? There was no conceivable way that Lady Henceforth would ever believe her stories of Laird's heroics now.

Anne sighed and looked down at the card the butler had just delivered to her.

It was only by a great gift of fortune that Lady Henceforth had witnessed Laird's one authentic rescue, since the rest of Anne's own tales were naught but froth and meringue. And fur. She cringed at the thought of them all.

Unfortunately, the most convincing evidence she could produce to support the fact that Laird had indeed changed—even though he had disproved the notion that very same night—was that he did not make love to her even when he knew she wanted nothing more at that moment.

Sadly, though, she could not share that choice bit of proof with anyone, and especially not with Lady Henceforth.

A dozen minutes later, the carriage in which Anne was riding passed a tall hedgerow, and Chasten Cottage burst into view.

She wrapped her gloved fingers over the top of the carriage door window and leaned her face out into the wind to watch the approach.

Coincidentally, another vehicle was just quitting Chasten Cottage, necessitating Anne's carriage to halt to allow its passage.

As it did, she caught sight of the lone gentleman passenger. He tipped his hat as the carriage rolled past. A shiver slid down her spine.

Anne leaned as far out of the half window as she could without falling, just to be sure of what she saw.

A steady wind blew in her face, making her eyes water, but the distinctive MacLaren coat of arms painted on the door of the town carriage was all the additional verification she needed.

Laird.

How could he do this?

She yanked her head back inside the cab and slammed her fist down upon the seat cushion.

The tears summoned by the breeze trickled down her cheek. Her fingers scrabbled inside her reticule for a handkerchief to dab them away.

She would not wish Lady Henceforth to believe she was crying, for indeed she was not. She wasn't crying at all.

The tears were from the wind . . . not because she had just seen her betrothed—her pretend betrothed—leaving his former fiancée's home. Certainly not.

Chapter 15

How to Take Tea

Taking tea with Lady Henceforth after seeing Laird leave her home put Anne in a very awkward situation, and did nothing to improve her mood.

"Dear Anne, I am so pleased that your fall from the cliff did not cause you any lingering injury." Lady Henceforth gifted her with a mawkish smile.

"Only a scratch. I was very, very fortunate that Laird came along when he did." Anne met Lady Henceforth's insipid smile with one matched in cloyingness.

She wondered whether she ought to mention that she had passed Laird on the road or pretend she was blissfully unaware that her husband-to-be had been paying a visit to the widow.

"Lady MacLaren seems very excited at the prospect of her son's wedding." Lady Henceforth poured the tea to the very brim of Anne's cup and carefully passed it to her.

"Yes, indeed." Distractedly, Anne reached out for the spilling dish of tea and settled it before her, not caring a bit if any dripped onto the polished top of the tea table.

On second thought, Anne mused, given that Lady Henceforth had sent the carriage to retrieve her from MacLaren Hall, and likely knew her and Laird's carriages would pass, another option would be to simply neglect mentioning the sighting at all and wait to see when, and in what context, the widow would offer the information.

Anne decided on the latter, given the widow's game with the too-full teacup. She waited, calmly managing to sip her tea and to chew her soggy lemon biscuit, for a report of the visit to eventually burst from her gloating hostess's mouth.

"When will the banns be posted?" Lady Henceforth began most innocently.

"Soon enough, I suppose. We haven't discussed the wedding plans yet. My sister Mary is in last months of her pregnancy, and travel for her would be most difficult." Anne smiled pleasantly. Best let Lady Henceforth feel she had time enough to snatch Laird back from her if that was what she intended.

Lud, wouldn't it be fortuitous if that was what the widow planned to do. Anne knew she ought to feel happy at the very likely prospect. But she did not.

"I remember when Laird—oh, you do not mind if I refer to him by his Christian name, do you?" Lady Henceforth was almost grinning. "It is how he asked me to refer to him, and therefore how I think of him."

"Oh, do not change your thinking because you fear offending me." Anne munched another bit of her biscuit.

"So." Lady Henceforth leaned over the petite tea table between them. "Are you quite in love?"

For some reason, that question struck Anne hard and tipped her from her footing. An ache akin to a too snug corset tightened in her chest.

"Or don't you know, Anne?" The far left edge of Lady Henceforth's mouth twitched in apparent anticipation of Anne's reply. "Have you even been in love before?"

"I have never felt this way before. *Ever*. When I see him, an excitement pulses through me. He makes me laugh. He makes me feel as though I am at my best when we are together . . . as though nothing is beyond my grasp." Anne touched her teacup to her lips, startled by her own words.

Lady Henceforth blinked, and she appeared utterly thunderstruck.

So Anne continued. "When we are apart, I feel like a piece of me is missing, and I only feel whole when we are together again. Until Laird, I did not know I was incomplete."

Lady Henceforth stared at Anne. "Oh."

It was evident that the widow did not expect to hear what Anne had told her. And, lud, until she said them, Anne had not expected the words, either.

Anne sat very still.

For every word she said . . . was true.

A flush of warmth shot up from between Anne's breasts, and she felt rather embarrassed at having bared her heart—for indeed that was what she had done—to Lady Henceforth, of all people.

"What about you, Lady Henceforth . . . for-give me, Constance?" Anne began. "You were married once, but I am worldly enough to know that most marriages in England are not love matches."

Lady Henceforth glanced down at her teacup and swirled the contents as she pondered the question. "I-I was in love, *once*.

"But it was a forbidden love." Lady Henceforth laughed tightly. "I have never admitted this." She looked up at Anne.

"I do apologize. I should not have asked." Anne stared over the rim of her teacup at the widow.

"I was in love. I knew all the feelings you had expressed and more." Lady Henceforth sighed forlornly. "But my parents had arranged a marriage for me. Lord Henceforth was much older than I. Closer to my grandfather's years than my own."

Anne grimaced. "You had no comment in the matter at all?"

"No. And so I had to bid my love a gentle adieu."

Anne sighed as well, finding unexpected poignancy in her story. "And did you ever see him again?"

Lady Henceforth shook her head. "No, Graham purchased a commission in the Fourteenth Light Dragoons soon afterward."

"*Graham?*" Anne bolted upright in her chair. "Graham Allan? Laird's brother?"

Lady Henceforth's eyes widened. "No, I said *he* purchased a commission. You misheard, Anne."

"No, I do not believe I did. You said *Graham.*"

Tears sprouted in Lady Henceforth's brown eyes. "No, I am certain you misheard." Looking suddenly afraid, she clutched her middle. "Anne, I do apologize, but I am not feeling well. I shall summon my carriage for you. We shall finish tea at another time, if you do not mind."

Anne was stunned. "No, of course I do not mind, Constance. Is there anything I can do for you?"

Lady Henceforth shook her head. "No. Good day, Anne."

"Found anything interesting to read yet?" Anne asked.

Laird whirled around, scattering the bundle of music he held onto the parquet floor. "I didn't hear you come in." He knelt down and began gathering up the sheet music. "How was your afternoon? You were not gone long."

"No, I wasn't. Lady Henceforth took ill quite suddenly." She stooped and started picking up the sheets alongside him. "How was she when you were there?" Anne did not look at him, but her hands stilled while she awaited his reply.

"Lady Henceforth had invited me for luncheon."

"Well, that accounts for it. So much food in such little time." Laird was unprepared for the stark sarcasm in Anne's voice.

"Anne." He eased his hand up her arm. "We are both working toward the same end. To repair my image in Lady Henceforth's eyes." He felt her flinch at that, and he wished with all he was that he not spoken those words.

Anne shrugged his hand from her shoulder and came to her feet. "This is the last room to be searched, I believe. No letters?"

Laird shook his head.

"I found one."

He turned and looked up to see Anne holding a folded sheet of foolscap. She held it out to him, and without removing his gaze from hers, he took it from her.

"I found it wedged in the back of a chest of drawers the other night—in Graham's bedchamber."

"What is this?" Laird rose slowly and took the letter from her hand.

"I do not know. I didn't read it. It was addressed to you."

With utmost reverence, Laird slowly opened the letter's creased folds and began to read the short missive. He grimaced as though a fist had closed around his heart.

"Laird?"

"*Oh my God.*" He clenched the letter in his hand and fled the room.

Chapter 16

How to Skip a Stone

Anne found Laird on a grassy slope beside the lake, sitting slumped against an oak tree.

His eyes were swollen and his face drawn, but as she walked toward him through the damp grass, he turned to look up at her, and his lips lifted.

Though she tried to harden herself to him, her heart softened, and the urge to reach out to him tugged at her arms. "I shouldn't have given you the letter. Whatever your brother had written upset you greatly." She knelt beside him and ran a soothing hand through his hair.

"No, Anne, you did exactly the right thing by giving me this letter. It changes so much. I only wish that someone had found it sooner."

Laird expelled a long breath. "I must thank my mother for lodging you in Graham's bedchamber. Had you not found this . . . I might never have known."

Anne shifted and sat on a grass tuft beside him, and together they stared out at the sun glistening on the glassy lake. After a few moments, she turned her gaze and glanced up at Laird. "There are several other unused bedchambers at the Hall. Why would she assign Graham's to me?"

"I think it is just as she claimed, you are family to her now." Laird wrapped his arms around his knees. "I am glad that she settled you in his chamber, and that you found the letter."

Anne plucked a piece of new green grass from the earth. "Will you tell me what it said that touched you so deeply?"

Laird sighed at that. He came to his feet and leaned against the oak's wide trunk. "My father always wished that I, as his heir, would follow his path in life. And I did for a time. But after I left Oxford, he purchased for me a fine commission in the cavalry. His years in the military had taught him discipline—something he believed I sorely lacked."

Anne tilted her head and looked up at him. "You, in the military. Following orders. All neat and tidy, standing in very straight lines." She shifted her gaze out over the sparkling water. "I am afraid I just cannot see it."

Laird laughed. "Nor could I. So when the first opportunity presented itself, I sold it."

"Oh dear. I do not expect that your father approved."

"It stirred him up until he became red about the gills, that's for certain, which, during my rebellious period, served to please me immensely."

Anne rocked forward on her toes, standing. She walked down to the lake's shore and crouched to find a round, smooth stone. "But Graham did join the dragoons; I believe Lady Henceforth mentioned it to me over tea."

"He did, and very suddenly, too." Laird came to stand beside Anne upon the muddy water's edge. "Not even my father knew his second son had indeed stepped into his oversized boots until Graham was packed off to the Peninsula."

"Your father must have been proud of Graham for taking the initiative and mirroring his grand career."

Laird shook his head dolefully. "He wasn't. It was his opinion that my brother's life was now in danger because he felt he had to fulfill the family duty—because *I* was too much of a coward to do it myself."

Anne turned her gaze up at Laird. "Your father actually said that to you?"

He shrugged his left shoulder. "Graham and I were very close. So Father knew just how to plunge the knife when he decided he wanted to hurt me." He paused for a long moment. "I never saw Graham again." Laird looked down and noticed that Anne was offering him a flat stone. He leaned to his side and skipped the stone, sending it across the lake along with the weighty memories that had plagued him for more than a year.

"That was very unfair of your father." Anne loosened another stone from the damp mud at the shore. She held it up to Laird.

But this time he clasped her wrist and hauled her to her feet. "But you, Anne, my absolutely mad darling, redeemed me with this letter."

"I?" Anne's mouth was still agape when he pulled her hand over her head and spun her in a tight circle. "Stop, stop, Laird." Her laugh tinkled like sleigh bells.

"Don't you see? Until this letter, I believed I was, as my father claimed, responsible for Graham's death. This letter frees me." Laird dropped Anne's hand and brought the letter to his lips and kissed it loudly.

"The letter . . . what does it say?" Anne rested her hands on her hips as she gathered her breath.

"In this letter, Graham admits that he purchased the commission because he had to leave St. Albans. The woman he loved was marrying a much older, wealthier man, and it pained him too greatly to remain." Laird's mouth curved into a wide grin. "Don't you see, Anne? Graham didn't sign over his life because I failed to meet Father's expectations. He was in love."

A dark curtain cloaked Anne's bright expression, and she became instantly silent.

"Anne? Is something wrong?"

"Nothing you need concern yourself over." Anne started hurriedly walking to the house.

"Anne!" Laird ran after her. Grabbing her hand, he whirled her into his arms to face him. "What is worrying you? What is it?" His mouth was only a hand's width from hers, and he knew he walked in dangerous territory.

"I . . .'tis nothing." Anne's cheeks colored as she tried to pull away.

"Anne, you are a terrible liar. God knows, it's not from lack of practice. *Please*." He tried to convince her with a light smile. "Nothing can blight my day now. The guilt of my brother's death has been lifted from my shoulders, by Jove."

"Lady Henceforth admitted something to me today—something I don't believe she intended to share." Anne chewed her bottom lip, and her brow furrowed deeply. "What she said makes me fairly certain that the woman your brother spoke of in his letter is . . . *she*."

"Constance?" Laird grew very still. His gaze searched Anne's own.

Anne nodded solemnly. "I believe so."

"Wh-what did she say?" he asked hesitantly.

"Laird, I may be wrong."

"Please. Tell me."

"All right. She that she had been in love with a young man, but her parents, on her behalf, accepted an offer from an elderly man—Lord Henceforth. And that the young man purchased a commission when he learned she was to marry Lord Henceforth."

"I heard not one word of this." Laird slowly lowered his hands to his sides. He was completely stunned, as though he'd taken a blow to the back of his head with a rifle butt.

"I am sorry. Perhaps I should not have mentioned anything . . . I only saw a connection where, I fully admit, there may be none at all." Anne reached a comforting hand out to Laird, but he took a step away, and her fingertips came away empty. "Laird, please forgive me. If you wish it, I will go to Chasten Cottage on the morrow and speak with Lady Henceforth to clear up this misunderstanding. I am sure that is all it was." Her cheeks flushed red, and she averted her gaze.

"No." Laird shook his head dully. "We both know you did not mistake her words."

Anne clearly did not comprehend the significance of a past love match between Lady Henceforth and his brother. His life might have been so different . . . if only he had known. The possibility of a relationship between the two certainly begged for some hard answers.

"I thank you for offering to spare me from

this, Anne, but I must speak with Constance myself. If she and my brother were in love, then I must question everything that I believe existed between us. Please, excuse me, Anne. I must go to Chasten Cottage. I have a question to ask, one that only Constance can answer."

Chapter 17

How to Gain Footing

A nne scraped a layer of mud from the soles of her boots, then sat down on the steps to unfasten the buttons and remove them before entering the house.

"Anne, my sweeting," Lady MacLaren called to her from the drawing room. "I am so glad you and Laird have returned from your walk. I saw you from my bedchamber window. Did you enjoy the view? The light on the water is so beautiful this time of day. Don't you agree?"

"Yes, Lady MacLaren, very much." Anne dangled her muddy boots behind her.

"A parcel arrived for you while you were out—from your sister, the Duchess of Blackstone." Lady MacLaren secured her needle into the woven silk stretched between the embroidery hoops, then peered around Anne into the entry passage beyond "Laird? A special messenger brought a letter for you—*from the House of Lords*." She waggled her brows proudly at Anne.

"The House of Lords?" Anne echoed. Oh, how she wished Laird were here to receive the letter . . . instead of heading across the fields to confront Lady Henceforth.

"Yes, what say you to that, son?" The countess's tone was buoyant with happiness. "The summons could not be better timed, eh?"

"Lady MacLaren, your son is not with me presently. He . . . decided on a ride and made a path straight to the stables rather than returning to the house." Anne's boots began to slip from her grip, and so she dropped a serviceable curtsy, with just enough bounce to regain purchase on the leather straps. "Do excuse me; I am excited to learn what my sister has sent." Anne started to turn to quit the room when Lady MacLaren called out to her again.

"He did not trot off to call upon Lady Henceforth again, did he?" Anne turned back to see a scowl twisting the countess's lips.

Anne opened her mouth, but then closed it

promptly. What use would adding another lie to her collection serve?

"He is betrothed to *you*, Anne. He ought not be seeing *that woman* at all."

"Truly, I do not mind." Anne glimpsed the parcel from her sister on the table near the door and slid a stocking-clad foot a few inches in that direction.

"Well, I do mind, and so should you." Lady MacLaren began to pace the drawing room with a stern, determined expression on her round face.

Anne slid her foot a few more inches. Just a little farther, and she could reach out and snatch up the parcel. She pointed her toe, and her foot began to move over the polished floor.

Oh good heavens. She tried to stop it, but it shot out from beneath her skirts. Anne waved the boots in her hand in wild circles to catch her balance. Her other hand scrambled for the drawing room door frame. Neither worked. Teetering backward, she slipped onto her backside.

"You know, dear, I have yet to arrange a proper betrothal ball for you and Laird—*in Town*." Lady MacLaren thrummed her fingertips on her lower lip. "What say you . . . we leave on the morrow for London?" Lady MacLaren whirled around, just as Anne managed to restore her footing and come to her feet.

London? Heat pricked at the backs of her eyes, though Anne wasn't quite sure why.

She should be thrilled to return to London. The letters weren't here, after all. And from the first, Lady Henceforth had brought her nothing but difficulty. She should be happy. Returning to London was without doubt the best thing for her given the wretched state of affairs.

"So what say you, Anne?" Lady MacLaren bobbed her head like a chicken, and Anne belatedly realized she wished Anne to do the same.

And so she did. "I think the idea is splendid."

"It is brilliantly timed, isn't it? We shall have two grand reasons to celebrate, the engagement and my dear son taking his rightful place in the House of Lords at last," she added cheerfully. "Oh, what am I doing dawdling like this? I should see to my packing right away." Lady MacLaren started for the doorway. "Solange! Solange, come at once!"

Before Lady MacLaren could reach the passage, Anne twirled and grabbed the parcel Mary had sent. She curled her toes, and using her nails for traction, lest she slip again, crept back across the entry hall for the staircase and her bedchamber above.

The moon had just taken its place in the darkening sky and the night air was cool to Anne's skin as she stood in the south garden breathing in the heady fragrance of a cluster of white flowers. She'd miss this garden. She'd miss MacLaren Hall and the countess. She'd even miss Laird.

Lud, she could not pretend any longer, though she wished she could. Once she returned to London, she would never return to St. Albans again.

Her life would never be the same.

Anne felt an aching emptiness in her heart, as if she were leaving her home and family forever. How odd that she should feel this way after so short a time. But she could not deny the force of her sense of loss.

The crunching of gravel and shells drew Anne's attention, and she looked over her shoulder toward the garden path. *Laird*. She knew this, felt his presence, even before he rounded the prickly hedge of holly and came into view.

"I didn't expect anyone to be in the garden at this hour," he said.

This did not fool Anne for a moment. He had come to the garden to find her.

"The house is abuzz with activity. It seems we're returning to London," he said.

Anne swung around to look directly at him. "You are going as well? Tomorrow?" The unintended exuberance in her voice brought a flush to her cheeks.

"Well, yes," he replied. Even in the soft moonlight, she could see that he was smiling.

He wasn't wearing a coat, or even a waistcoat. His lawn shirt was open at the throat and his doeskin breeches were tucked into his Hessian boots. He looked as though he had just come back from a very long, hard ride—although Anne knew Chasten Cottage was only a clutch of minutes from MacLaren Hall.

She wrenched her gaze from him, thankful her shrewish thoughts had not solidified into hurtful words.

"Your mother is planning a betrothal ball." She plucked a pale blossom, and raising it to her nose, sniffed deeply.

"I heard. But my haste in returning to Town

supersedes my mother's social inclinations."

She raised her eyes to his. "What do you mean by that?"

"I received a Writ of Summons. I have been commanded to attend Parliament and take my father's seat."

"You deserve it, Laird." Anne smiled at him. "You are worthy of the responsibility."

"My father would have never agreed."

Anne walked toward him. "But your father is gone—and he was wrong about you."

"Are you so sure?" Laird looked away from her. She lifted her hand to his jaw and turned his face to her. He needed to hear what she had to say.

"Yes. Don't you understand? He likely blamed you for his own faults because he could not accept his own weaknesses."

"How could you know this?"

"Because I have been invisible nearly all my life. I've watched people, learned from them, and over the years, I have come to understand that those who hate, who criticize, who blame with fervor, are in truth punishing others for the faults they see in themselves." Anne lowered her hand from his face and grasped Laird's hands in her own. "Your father had risen to great power in the House of Lords, but then, likely due to his own overweening pride and ambition, it slipped away from him. A man like that is bound not to accept his own failure in politics, and so, perhaps, he set his eye on grooming you, a bright young man, to succeed where he had failed."

"I told you once before, I could never meet his expectations."

"Of course not; no one could. Even he couldn't meet his own lofty requirements of himself. Laird, you were not to blame for his failures in government. You were not to blame for Graham heading off to war, or even for being jilted by Lady Henceforth." Without meaning to, Anne gave him a single shake, needing to make him understand, needing for him to believe her. "You are a good man. A gentleman. And if anyone can restore the proud MacLaren name in Parliament and in society, it is *you*."

"I have never had anyone believe in me as you do, Anne." Laird's eyes were swimming, but he chuckled quietly. "I would not be surprised if you somehow arranged for the Writ of Summons to be issued just now."

"Oh no. If a string was pulled, it would be

by Apsley, would it not?" Anne grinned. "This summons was a piece of the supposed wager, wasn't it? You take your father's seat in Parliament ... and become betrothed. I think those were the terms."

Laird laughed and waved his index finger in the air. "No, darling, I believe I was to marry before the end of the season and take my father's seat. I have done neither—*yet*."

"Ah, but you will." Anne turned from him, not wanting to face him as she spoke her next words. "Lady Henceforth no longer seems to find you an unfit match. Truth to tell, after speaking with her yesterday, I think she has it in her mind to nudge me out of her way. But that will not be so difficult, will it, since she was always your intended in this scheme?" She heard him come up fast behind her then, and bit her lower lip in nervous anticipation.

He grasped her shoulders and spun her around to face him. His eyes were deadly serious, his grip firm, and Anne knew he would not release her until he had responded.

"Anne." Even in the moonlight, his eyes burned like the cobalt center of a flame. "What is it *you* want?"

She averted her gaze and stared off at a cluster of vines in the distance, trying very hard not to choke on the emotions congealing around her words. "What a ridiculous question, my lord. You know all too well that my only wish is to be free of these lies."

Laird lifted his hand from one of her shoulders, cupped her chin, and turned her face to his. His eyes seemed to search hers.

But it was the truth.

Heat pricked and seared the backs of her eyes, so she squeezed her lids closed.

Anne couldn't pretend to be Laird's betrothed any longer. She was so . . . "So tired of pretending."

"Then don't pretend."

Anne's eyes flicked open. She hadn't meant to say that.

Laird released his hold on her, allowing her to step away, flee into the garden if that was what she wished.

She stood before him, unmoving. Her head tilted upward to look into his dark eyes. Anne had seen him look at her in that questioning way only once before . . . in the library.

And by degrees, it became clear to her what he was doing just now—he was asking her to decide what she really wanted. Asking her if she wanted him.

She lowered her chin, thinking as she inhaled a deep fortifying breath into her lungs. Then, her decision made, Anne stepped forward.

His arms came around her body and held her tight. She fell against him, felt his mouth against her throat.

Suddenly, he lifted Anne in the air and whirled her around, laying her gently in a bed of perfumed white blossoms.

Anne braced herself for the full weight of him to move over her, but he settled a hand just over each of her shoulders and gently lowered his body to hers, his mouth to her lips.

His wet tongue skimmed her lips, and she obligingly parted them, inviting him inside. It was the sweetness of brandy she expected to taste, but she didn't. Instead she reveled in the heat of his mouth. All she smelled was a light, smoky maleness.

He shifted his weight and laid alongside her. "No more pretending—either of us."

Anne nodded and caught his shoulder. She pulled him closer.

"I've wanted nothing so much in my life, Anne, as I want you now." Laird grabbed a handful of her green taffeta gown and pulled it high about her hips.

She squirmed, and then she felt his hands moving again, almost touching her . . . yes, touching her now. Slowly, so softly.

"Oh!" Her hips bucked as his hand slid through the furl of her womanhood and found her core. His thumb centered there and caressed her in slow circles, making her arch and press against his hand.

His breath was suddenly hot about her chest. He caught the ribbon at her bodice between his teeth and tugged until the taffeta parted. He unfastened her chemise.

The night air was cool on her breasts, and when his teeth nipped at each of her rose peaks, it almost hurt, but not quite. Her nipples throbbed now.

"*Laird.*" She was mindless with pleasure. A surge of heat built mercilessly between her quivering thighs as he kissed and sucked and caressed her.

He felt hot and hard as stone against her hip, and so Anne rolled just enough that her far hand could reach him there. She fumbled to open his fall, lowering the fabric to allow her fingers inside. Hesitantly she took him into her hand.

She didn't know quite what to do. Still, when she guided him, hard and pulsing, from the fabric cocoon and into the air, she heard him gasp.

Boldly exploring him with her fingers, she grasped him firmly and ran her hand down his long length, and then back up again, squeezing the thick tip.

Laird thrust his head back, and the cords that ran down either side of his neck grew taut.

She caught his shoulder to urge him over her, spreading her legs so that he might move between them.

How she wanted to feel his body against hers, feel his weight upon her, feel him taking her, filling her. He leaned back, and while balancing himself on his knees, knelt between her thighs, and whisked his lawn shirt off.

Reaching up, she touched the mounds of his chest, and then trailed her fingers down to the muscles carved into his abdomen. "Laird, I do not pretend now. I want you." She slid her hands up to his jaw and drew him to her. She kissed his lips, but still she felt him trying to pull back.

She could smell his need for her, and she knew he could feel the growing dampness between her own legs. "Please, Laird."

"I want you, Anne, so much." At last he eased over her. He leaned back for an instant, and his hands were lifting her hips to him. Slowly he pushed forward, until just the thick, plum-shaped tip of him nudged between her woman's lips.

She bucked her hips against him. He was almost inside her—almost. The heat of his engorged tip pushed inside . . . yes . . . but then he pulled back. Another thrust. Anne twisted and pushed down on him. Yes . . . *this* time.

He spread her legs wider then, and she felt his thumb against her again. Circling, making her toes curl as he thrust his hardness into her, just a little deeper each time.

It was maddening.

He lifted his hand away from her cleft and leaned over her stomach to kiss her mouth at the very moment he slammed into her depths.

She gasped as he thrust and rocked into her again and again. No more gentle prodding. No more long, slow strokes. He was moving into her . . . touching her everywhere . . . sucking at her nipples, pushing so deep . . . kissing her.

Her fingertips dug into the taut muscles of his broad shoulders, and she held on as his rhythm grew faster and he pounded into her.

Her thighs were quivering uncontrollably now. The coiled tightness below was unbearable. She gripped him with her thighs as best she could, just in time.

Fire seems to burst from where he touched her, radiated down her limbs, pulsing. She squeezed her eyes tight and cried out.

A wash of heat skimmed his skin suddenly, and she felt his muscles contract as he pumped his seed into her. A cool moistness broke over his back as he collapsed atop her. Then he turned his head and kissed her throat.

Anne was drained and undeniably exhausted, but . . . thoroughly, giddily happy. She couldn't help the smile that spread across her face.

Laird kissed into her throat again, and then he propped himself on his elbow and gazed down at her. She couldn't hide her silly smile and didn't even try.

The edge of Laird's mouth twitched upward, the way she'd come to realize it did whenever he was about to say something amusing. He lifted his brow innocently. "You weren't . . . *pretending*, were you?"

Anne threw her weight against him, hitting his shoulder and knocking him onto his back. She rolled on top of him and kissed his mouth. "Well, I am known for my acting abilities."

Chapter 18

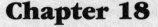

How to Be Utterly Convincing

The emptiness that Anne had felt when she first entered the garden was all but a forgotten memory now. Everything was different. She had changed, for suddenly her future was as clear and bright as the morning sun streaming through the bedchamber window.

It was a new day and her future was with Laird.

Oh, they hadn't discussed it, but she knew. She felt it.

There would be no more pretending. No more lies. It was a morning of new beginnings for both of them.

Solange slipped the last pin into Anne's hair and had just turned to close the portmanteau when the parcel Mary had sent caught Anne's eye. "Oh, mustn't forget Father's *Book of Maladies and Remedies*!" She whirled, snatched it up, and tossed it into her leather portmanteau.

"You do not wish to bring it with you inside the carriage?" Solange asked. "It is a long drive to London; you might wish for something to read."

Anne laughed. "I might indeed, but believe me, this book is not something I ever intend to read."

She spun in a circle, happier and more content than she could ever remember being in her entire life.

Berkeley Square
That evening

"It wasn't nearly as difficult as I had imagined it would be." Anne threw herself on her bed and stared up at the ceiling as she spoke to her sister Elizabeth. "Actually, I think I am rather good at playing a countess-to-be."

"Yes, I am sure you had grand time tottering about MacLaren Hall, but Anne, that is not why you were there. Did you bother looking for the letters at all while you were playing countess?"

"Countess-to-be." Anne rolled over on her side and propped herself up on her elbow. "Lord MacLaren and I have not exchanged our vows, Elizabeth."

"Oh, right. I had quite forgotten," her sister said quite sarcastically. "And when is the blessed day?"

"Well, we have not determined the date yet, but I expect we will take care of that detail after the betrothal ball." Anne knew she was chattering, but so much had happened since she left London, and, la, she hadn't been able to speak freely about everything with anyone in St. Albans.

Elizabeth sat down on the edge of bed and looked over her shoulder at Anne. "You are teasing me about the ball, aren't you?"

Anne sat up. "Oh *no*. Lady MacLaren spoke of nothing else during the entire journey from St. Albans to Mayfair. She claims that this ball will be her claim to society immortality. The *ton* will have seen nothing like it—at least outside of St. James's Palace, and she wasn't entirely certain about that. The arrangements are still in the making, you see."

"So how will you do it? You must have had

plenty of time to rehearse." Elizabeth's eyes were widening with anticipation.

"How will I do . . . what?"

"Cry off, you goose! Will you do it after the ball, or before? Oh, please say after, Anne."

"What a thing to say! If I were to cry off before there would be no reason for a betrothal ball, now would there?"

Elizabeth laughed. "Why, you are so practical I think I might mistake you for our sister Mary."

"Besides, I am not going to cry off." Anne opened her portmanteau and tossed the partially unwrapped book Mary had sent, onto the bed.

Elizabeth completely ignored the heavy tome that had landed beside her. "What did you say, Anne—that you are not going to withdraw from the engagement?"

"That's right. I have decided that I rather like the idea of being Laird's wife. And once I became used to the attention, it was not so difficult to endure. Sometimes I have even enjoyed it."

"But . . . I thought Lady Henceforth, and everyone who attended the ball at MacLaren Hall—which must have been half of London society—believes Lord MacLaren has reformed and is now a perfect gentleman."

"Yes. It took some doing, but between the two of us, Laird and I, that is, we were able to convince them that he has redeemed himself." Anne lifted a brow. "He even received a Writ of Summons to appear at Parliament and take his seat."

"I do not understand. Why are you refusing to cry off? It makes no sense at all to me."

"Well, it makes perfect sense to me. I will not cry off . . . *because I love him.*"

"You *love* Lord MacLaren?" Elizabeth stared at Anne for moment and then laughed. "Oh, Anne, you had me believing you there."

"This is not folly, Elizabeth." Anne met her sister's gaze with a serious look of her own. "I love him."

Elizabeth slid to the edge of the bed and came slowly to her feet. "Gads, you are being serious. You really do love him."

"I do." A gentle smile formed on Anne's mouth. "I really do. He is a good man, with a kind heart. He worked so hard to prove that he didn't need anyone, didn't need love, that I was unaware of his true character and heart. But now that I have, I want to spend my life with him."

"Does he know how you feel?" Concern was plain in Elizabeth's eyes.

"Yes." Anne smiled at the memory of last night in the south garden. "He knows."

Cockspur Street
The library

Apsley shook his head so fiercely that his brandy sloshed over the lip of the crystal glass he was holding. "No, I don't believe you, MacLaren. This is some clever way to renege on our wager, isn't it?"

"We never had a true wager. If I remember correctly, and I do admit that night was somewhat of a blur to me, my mother interrupted before the bet was made." Laird laughed and sat down in the chair opposite Apsley. "But to prove to you that this is not folly, set your stakes now, and the day I claim Anne as my wife, I will pay you."

"Hardly convincing. There is a catch to your offer. I just have not yet determined your strategy." Apsley swirled the brandy in his glass.

"There is no strategy, I swear it. I have fallen in love with her and I believe she loves me as well. And so, if she will have me, I will marry her at St. George's at our earliest convenience."

"Then you have not yet asked her to marry you."

Laird grinned. "What, are you telling me that I am supposed to *ask* her to marry me? I just can't proclaim us betrothed?"

"All right, fair enough." Apsley laughed for a moment, but then the expression on his face grew very serious. "You really love her?"

"Yes, I do."

"Now, we are not speaking of Lady Henceforth, are we?"

"*No.* I was mistaken about her." The muscles along Laird's jaw tightened.

"Now, now, no need to get yourself so worked up. I had to ask."

"I do not love Constance. In fact, I don't believe I ever did. I think my wish to marry her was driven more by a desire for respectability than anything else." Laird exhaled. "But Anne . . . Christ, I never thought I would feel this way. When I am with her, I am a better man. She makes me feel that I have it within me to do anything."

"Damn me, I've never seen you this way."

"I've never felt this way." Laird knew he was grinning like a fool, but he didn't care. He was in love. *Love*.

"So . . . just to be clear, we are speaking of the chit who sneaked into your bedchamber to steal a bundle of secret letters—*correct*?"

"Apsley, you are trying my patience. Yes, Miss Anne Royle." Laird leaned his head against the rest and looked down his nose at Apsley. "And about those letters . . . truth to tell, old man, I don't know that they ever existed. Might be a story tossed out there by the Tories to discredit the prince."

"You may be right there." Apsley nodded his head, considering the notion. "But you know, I can't help but think that Lord Lotharian knows more than he is telling. Word is, he was a friend to both Prinny and your father when he was a Whig. No one can read the old gambler, he's so bloody good. They say he knows a man's soul from the very first moment he meets him—and yet he only allows others to see what he wishes them to see."

"So what are you saying, Apsley, that this effort to find the letters is part of some grander machination set in motion by Lotharian?" Laird shook his head. "I don't see the bank, Apsley. Other than helping to prove or disprove the Royle sisters' lineage, how would Lotharian profit from such an elaborate ruse?"

"I don't think he means to personally benefit at all. I think he always meant for Anne to benefit. I think when he and the Old Rakes sent her into your bedchamber, they knew you were already there. They meant for you to catch her."

"Oh, Apsley, my fellow, you have had far too much to drink this night." Laird came to his feet and walked across the room. Absently he peered out the window.

He looked back over his shoulder at Apsley. "So your theory is that my deciding, just this night, to marry Anne was somehow preordained? Preposterous."

"No, you are right. Far too much would be dependent on chance for Lotharian to have had anything to do with it. Word at White's is that he risks nothing."

"Exactly."

Apsley exhaled, then struggled to his feet and headed for the brandy decanter. "Not having any tonight?" He raised his eyebrows as he waved the bottle in the air.

"Not tonight." Laird had too much to think about just now.

Berkeley Square

It was not yet dawn when Elizabeth flung herself forward and sat bolt upright in her bed. A droplet of cool sweat rolled down her neck to her collarbone, then over the swell of her breast to trickle down into the valley at her bosom.

She closed her eyes and struggled to steady her breathing. She'd had another dream, the sort that came true . . . at least half of the time.

Crawling from her bed, she padded to her washbasin. She splashed her face with a little water and stood over the basin. She blinked the moisture from her eyes and let the water drip from the edge of her jaw into the basin.

In her dream, Anne had been holding a large sheet of vellum in her hands. Elizabeth couldn't see exactly what it was, but she knew, somehow, that Anne had found something of great importance in their quest to learn their heritage. Something *very* important. And then, suddenly, her dream shifted. Her sister was laughing and happier than Elizabeth had ever seen her before. She was dancing in Lord MacLaren's embrace, as Lady MacLaren and countless others looked on approvingly.

Elizabeth held her breath, hoping to slow her heart's pounding inside her chest. How she wished the dream had ended there, but it hadn't.

For suddenly the images had grown disturbing.

Apsley walked by what Elizabeth thought to be Carlton House on Pall Mall just as the bells somewhere in the distance tolled noon hour. She heard the clop of horses on the road. Then she saw Apsley turn, and suddenly Elizabeth was screaming—a horrible, bone-chilling cry. Then the image had jerked suddenly to another night. Now Anne stood in the middle of a ballroom, tears streaming down her face, and Elizabeth could not reach her sister, no matter how hard she tried. And then everything was dark, save the orange spikes of fire in a hearth as a woman's slender hand fed paper into the flames.

Elizabeth dropped down into the wooden chair beside her washstand. Her chemise was damp and sticking to her skin. She pinched it and pulled it away as she pondered the meaning of the dream.

But try as she might, Elizabeth could not decipher what she had seen. There was no logical order to it. Too many pieces of this puzzling dream were missing or distorted.

All Elizabeth knew was that something devastating was going to happen to Anne, and that there was nothing she would be able to do to stop it.

Her older sister Mary would have chided her for wasting money, but Elizabeth had already exhausted too much time coming to the decision to track Apsley. After all, she did not even know if the event she'd seen in her dream would happen today—if at all . . . and then there was her macabre scream. She shivered every time she thought of its ghastly sound.

By the time she had finished her tea and had scanned the morning newspaper for any mention of an accident on Pall Mall yesterday, hailing a hackney was Elizabeth's only option if she wished to arrive at Carlton House's entrance on Pall Mall before noon.

She slid a crepe mantle around her shoulders

and plopped a large straw bonnet down upon her head. A glance in the passageway mirror confirmed the utility of the bonnet. She'd only need to tilt her head, and the wide brim would conceal her face from view. *Perfect*.

As the hackney drew up before Carlton House, Elizabeth reached into her brocade reticule and withdrew the gold watch that had belonged to her father. She flipped open the case. Two minutes until noon. Snapping the watch closed, she flipped a coin to the hackney driver and stepped out onto the pathway lining Pall Mall.

She stood against the column-lined fence and peered past the guardsman, through the arched entrance to Carlton House. The only windows she could see facing Pall Mall were nearly at the roofline, making it impossible to see inside the royal residence. Still, she squinted and tried to peer in, wondering if the regent was at home. Who knew, maybe at that very moment the Prince of Wales was looking down to the street, wholly unaware that the young woman in the wide straw bonnet standing at the archway might be his very own daughter.

A bell began to toll in the distance. The hammer of its striker hit the bronze skirt of the bell several times before the sound's significance dawned on Elizabeth. She walked a few steps toward the road and glanced to the left.

There he was—Apsley. He headed toward her now.

Elizabeth turned her body, intending to conceal herself as best she could near the guarded arch entrance. She kept her eyes on Apsley as she rushed toward the arch. The twelfth reverberation of the bell clock faded gradually, and only then did Elizabeth hear the thunder of hoof falls coming from the archway. She wrenched her head around just in time to register a huge gleaming carriage and six bearing down on her.

A horrified scream rose up inside her throat and rent the air. Something slammed into her ribs, knocking the air from her lungs. She hit the pavers hard, and sparkles of light filled her head.

"Elizabeth? Answer me, gel. Come on now."

Blinking her eyes, she focused on the face hovering a breath from her own nose. *Apsley*.

She opened her mouth to speak when a young woman's familiar visage appeared over her. "Is she injured?" the woman asked.

Oh, criminy. It could not be.

Elizabeth swallowed hard as she stared at the pair of concerned, large blue eyes peering down at her. The woman's hair was golden-hued, not quite brown but not flaxen like Anne's at all. Her skin was fair, quite pale actually. Perhaps it was because she was so close, but it seemed to Elizabeth that the woman's nose was rather long, but delicate, too, and decidedly aristocratic. No, there was no question about the young woman's identity—it was Princess Charlotte.

Apsley offered Elizabeth a hand and helped her to sit upright, but Elizabeth never took her gaze from the young woman.

"Are you injured?" the woman asked her directly.

Elizabeth nodded. "No, Your Royal Highness."

Apsley helped Elizabeth to her feet and bent to retrieve her straw bonnet.

Elizabeth's ribs ached fiercely, and her breathing had not completely returned to normal. She was stunned. But not from Apsley's daring rescue of her before she was crushed beneath hoof and wheel of the carriage. She stared, wide-eyed, at the princess, searching for any familial similarities. It was because . . . la, Princess Charlotte might very well be her half sister! It was certainly possible—even likely.

She brought her hand to her mouth to hush the excited laughter bursting forth.

"I am glad that you are unhurt." Princess Charlotte laid a gentle hand on Elizabeth's arm and peered hard at her. "Are we acquainted, miss?"

"Miss Elizabeth Royle, Your Royal Highness." Belatedly she dipped into her proper curtsy to honor her.

Princess Charlotte gave a questioning glance to an older woman standing at her side. "Is she—?"

The other woman nodded.

An amused smile came upon the princess's pink lips. "You are not yet known to me, but dear Miss Royle, today has changed that. I am very pleased to know you at last."

At last? Elizabeth was so stunned, she could not manage any sort of verbal reply, and so she bobbed another serviceable curtsy.

"Good day, Miss Royle." Her Royal Highness spun on blue silk slippers and was handed up into her carriage.

A crack of a whip started the team of glossy

ebony horses forward, and within a moment, the carriage had quit Pall Mall and had turned onto Cockspur Street.

Elizabeth watched until she could no longer see the dust kicked up from the carriage wheels, and then faced Apsley. "Thank you, dear sir, for snatching me from the path of the carriage."

Apsley shrugged. "You are most welcome, though I daresay, Miss Elizabeth, you might have at least acknowledged me to Princess Charlotte."

Elizabeth gasped. "Oh dear me."

Apsley laughed. "Perhaps someday you will have another chance. She may be your sister, after all, no?"

"Yes, that's true. And now we have met."

Apsley began to chatter on, but Elizabeth barely heard him at all. She was too confused.

Why had her dream frightened her so, when the outcome was probably the most amazing and exciting event of her life?

"Allow me to escort you home, Miss Elizabeth." Apsley offered Elizabeth his arm and warily guided her across the street. "I've always been fortunate enough to find a hackney at the Opera House. He stepped to the edge of the pavers and tipped his hat toward an approaching hackney. "Oh, oh, see there? What did I tell you? I excel at finding exactly what I need precisely when I need it." He grinned charmingly at her as he passed her up into the cab.

"Yes, I expect you do." Elizabeth leaned toward Apsley as he took his seat across from her. "Would you please ask the driver to hasten his way to Berkeley Square? I cannot contain my excitement much longer."

Apsley chuckled and rapped knuckles on the front of the cab, and the hackney lurched forward. "Eager to tell everyone that MacLaren is not the only hero about?"

"Oh, heavens no." Elizabeth shook her head fiercely. "I must tell everyone that I met my *sister* . . . I mean . . . Princess Charlotte."

"Oh, that." Apsley looked positively crestfallen. "Jolly good."

Chapter 19

How to Read Between the Lines

Berkeley Square
Late that afternoon

"**D**ear Elizabeth, I know you were thrilled to meet Princess Charlotte, but please, let Anne speak." Lady Upperton sighed. "We have yet to hear about what she found at Mac-Laren Hall."

"But you don't understand," Elizabeth huffed. "It did not strike me at first, because I was stunned by our meeting, but I realize now that Princess Charlotte looks nothing like me. Nothing like *any* of us. I am beginning to wonder if she truly is my half sister at all."

"Well, gel, you do not resemble Prinny, either. Be thankful for that," Gallantine teased.

Elizabeth scowled. "He may be our father, so please be considerate of our feelings, my lord."

"Elizabeth, Princess Charlotte resembles her mother, Caroline, far more so than the Prince of Wales," Anne explained. "Whether or not we bear any similarity of countenance is of no consequence. Even if you were a walking mirror image of the princess, the fact remains that we have no proof of our lineage."

"You are correct, Anne. We *still* have no proof. You should not have bothered traveling to St. Albans." Elizabeth grabbed a book from the Sheraton table and sat down in the window seat.

"Elizabeth, I would not have agreed to go to MacLaren Hall with the countess if I did not believe that the letters were hidden there. But they weren't." Anne looked at the three Old Rakes, lined up shoulder to shoulder on the drawing room's petite settee.

"And you searched the library especially well?" Lady Upperton asked.

"The library, oh yes. Every book, every crevice." Anne felt the blood begin to creep into her cheeks.

Lady Upperton lifted her lorgnette and peered

closely at Anne. "I expect he owned a desk. Did you check it?"

"Yes, yes! *Especially* the desk." Anne raised her hands in defeat. "In fact, we were seen in the library so many times supposedly searching for something interesting to read that it became a joke between us. I even wrote to Mary, asking her to please send me something for I could not seem to find what I was looking for in the library."

Elizabeth looked up from the text she was reading in the muted light from the window. "She must have had a merry chuckle when she sent Anne Father's dreary *Book of Maladies and Remedies*." She held it up for everyone to see. "It is so dull, even Father did not read every page."

"How do you know that, my sweet?" Lady Upperton asked, more out of politeness than interest, it seemed to Anne.

"Because several of the pages haven't been cut. See here?" Elizabeth fanned the pages, and just as she had said, more than a dozen double pages toward the end of the book had yet to be separated with a page cutter for reading. "Boring."

Something about the book caught Lord Lo

tharian's eye and he leapt up, which for a man of his years was quite impressive, Anne thought.

"Let me see the book, please." Lotharian met Elizabeth midway across the drawing room and quickly took the book from her. He ran his fingers along the edges of the pages. "No, the pages have *all* been cut open—but some have been sealed back together for some reason. That's damned odd, isn't it?"

He returned to the settee and opened the book for everyone to see. "Look here. One of the sealed pairs of pages is thicker than the others— 341 and 344."

"What did you say?" Anne stiffened.

"Just the page numbers, Anne," Lilywhite told her, "341 and 344."

Anne whirled around and met Elizabeth's own shocked stare directly. "Get the page cutter!"

Elizabeth raced from the drawing room and returned a moment later with the ivory blade Lotharian had stolen from beneath the floorboard hiding place in Laird's bedchamber. She handed it to Anne.

Anne scanned the etchings on the cutter until she found what she was looking for. "Here it is.

'BOMAR 342.' *Book of Maladies and Remedies* . . . page 342."

Lady Upperton clasped her hand to her heart. "Could it be that we've had the letters all along, but didn't know? Hurry, Lotharian, cut the pages! Cut them!"

Anne handed the ivory blade to Lotharian and cupped her hand over her mouth lest she squeal with excitement.

"Clear the settee." He flicked his hands outward and to his sides, as a maestro might. "Give me room, for God's sakes." Lotharian flipped up his coattails and reseated himself.

Anne held her breath as he carefully lowered the blade and inserted it into a small gap between the spine and page pairing. He slid the blade along the sealed bottom of the page.

"Mary was always thumbing through this book," Elizabeth blurted.

Lotharian's hand froze in place.

Elizabeth exhaled in frustration. "Well, why did she not notice that the top and bottom of this page were sealed when the others are not?"

"Hush, gel!" Gallantine snapped. "Lotharian needs silence so he does not slice whatever is hidden inside."

Lotharian gave a frustrated sigh. "Because, sometimes the glue in the spine can spread when the book is bound. And I am sure your sister was focusing on Royle's notes in the margins rather than the binding glue." He huffed. "Now, if everyone is finished chattering, I should like to learn what is between the pages."

Instantly, everyone became silent. No one spoke. No one moved, and for several moments, no one even breathed as Lotharian finished his incision.

He paused then and raised the book up to Anne. "You saw the notation on the blade. Go ahead. You do the honors, my dear. Reach inside."

Anne's hands trembled as she took the book and slipped her fingers between the pages. She looked at everyone in the room one by one, then inhaled a deep breath and grasped what was inside.

It was very thick; vellum, she guessed. Hardly what most people would use for a letter, but then the prince was not most people, was he?

Her heart pounded as she withdrew the paper.

It was vellum, but not a letter.

Even folded several times as it was, she could see the horizontal lines running across the paper.

Her hands shook wildly. "I can't. Lotharian, please, will you open it?" She held it out to him.

He did not reply, but took the vellum and opened it. Beads of sweat broke across his brow. "My God," he muttered.

"What is it?" Elizabeth cried. "Tell us, else I think I shall faint this very instant!"

Lotharian's gaze met Lady Upperton's and remained there.

"It's the register, isn't it?" she asked, but it was clear she already knew the answer.

He nodded, still too stunned to speak.

Lilywhite took the vellum from his hands and ran his finger over it in the air until he found what he was looking for. "Do you know what this is?" he asked Anne and Elizabeth.

They both shook their heads.

"Please, won't someone tell us?" Anne begged.

Lotharian finally spoke then. "It is the marriage register that the Prince of Wales and Maria Fitzherbert signed . . . on their wedding day."

Elizabeth's eyebrows drew close. "Is that all? A register? But this doesn't prove our heritage. Where are the letters?"

"The letters may no longer exist, I fear," Gallantine told her, laying a comforting hand across her shoulders.

"I think this is the evidence of the prince's illegal marriage that MacLaren somehow obtained. When hidden, the passing of the bill to name the Prince Regent became possible."

"But why would our father have hidden the register for the old MacLaren?" Anne asked. "All MacLaren possessed was the cutter, with the location of the register. Not the register itself. I don't understand."

"MacLaren and Royle were bosom friends for a time," Lilywhite told her. "We all were."

"But that doesn't explain—" Elizabeth interrupted.

"Perhaps, Dove, it was because your father was already the keeper of one potentially treasonous secret—you three gels—the prince's secret daughters with his morganatic wife, Maria Fitzherbert." Lady Upperton shrugged her shoulders. "We may never know why your father hid the register."

"And the register, when ... it is revealed?" Anne asked.

Lotharian grew darkly somber and serious. "*If* revealed—or if the prince learns the register has been found and considers it to be a threat to the monarchy, for indeed, he and Mrs. Fitzherbert have concealed their union from the people for many years—the simple possession of such politically damaging evidence could be deemed by the Crown ... *treason*."

"And possessing this register now—are we in danger?" Elizabeth was trembling with worry and dread.

"I don't know, dear." Lady Upperton slid her tiny body down from her chair. "But it is a possibility. To protect ourselves, and your futures, no one must know of this. No one!"

"B-but, I must at least tell Laird—Lord Mac-Laren." Anne grasped Lady Upperton's hand and pleaded with her. "He is about to take his seat in the House of Lords. This could jeopardize everything. He must know. I must tell him what we've found! He's been involved every step of the way."

"No, dear. At worst, everyone who knows of the register's existence could be implicated in a plot to commit treason if the Crown decided that is what should be done. It has happened before, at the prince's whim."

"At best, no one learns that we have the marriage register—until we have enough evidence—to solidly prove your heritage," Lotharian added. "Either way, you must remain silent about what we have discovered this night, Anne."

Lady Upperton hugged Anne to her. "If you care about him, and I suspect you do, do not put an end to his days in the House of Lords before they have yet to begin. You cannot let him know."

Anne nodded dully. She could not deny it, though she wished with all of her heart that she could. Lady Upperton was right. As much as she was loath to believe it, she felt the truth of her warning with every fiber of her being.

After everything she and Laird had overcome to find their way into each other's arms, into each other's hearts, his father's wrath had reached out for him again.

Through her.

Laird finally had redeemed himself in his own heart. After years of being told he accounted for nothing, Laird finally believed his own worth.

And now this disaster.

A cold realization snaked over Anne. Her legs seemed to lose their ability to support her, and she crumpled onto the settee alongside Lady Upperton.

"Dear child, come here," the old woman crooned.

Tears sprouted in Anne's eyes, and she buried her face in Lady Upperton's comforting arms.

She had involved Laird far too deeply already.

She had no choice now.

If she truly loved Laird, no matter how it tore at her, Anne knew what she must do. Her course was clear.

She had to cry off.

Chapter 20

How to Dance Like There
Is No Tomorrow

Two weeks later

Bored and impatient, Elizabeth paced Anne's bedchamber, having naught else to do but admire the swish and flutter of her own emerald-hued silk ball gown.

Lady Upperton's carriage was due to collect them both in less than half an hour. Cherie was attending to Anne's long golden tresses, but her sister had yet to even choose which of the two gowns lying on her tester bed she would wear. They were going to be late to her sister's own betrothal ball at Almack's.

"I do not know why you are fretting so, Anne. Lud, it is your second betrothal ball in as many weeks. No matter what you wear, you will look beautiful. There is no reason to give in to your nerves."

"You are well aware why I worry, and that it has nothing to do with my choice of gowns. You know what I must do, though God in heaven, I wish that I did not." Anne held a jewel-tipped hairpin up to Cherie, who plucked it from her fingers and sank it into a coil of flaxen curls. Anne reached for another pin from the tiny silver bowl atop her dressing table, but Elizabeth stilled her hand.

"You are going to cry-off this night?"

"I have tried to go to him for a fortnight, but I do not have the strength to break his heart. I must do it tonight before he announces our betrothal to all." Anne sucked in a staggered breath.

"We'll lock the register away and will never speak of it. You do not have to tell him . . . or anyone about its existence. You do not have to withdraw from the engagement!"

"Someday you will have a change of heart, Elizabeth." Though she tried to conceal it, Anne's eyes glistened with unshed tears. "Someday more evidence about our parents will be found and together the pieces will complete the puzzle of our heritage. The register will surface. I will not allow Laird to be implicated in a treasonable offense because of me."

"But, Anne, if you love him, do not do this. Do not cry off."

A single tear trickled down Anne's cheek. "I do this because I love him, Elizabeth. Because I love him so very much." She sniffled, and Cherie handed her a handkerchief. "Please, Elizabeth, wait for me in the drawing room. I promise I shan't be long. I just need a few moments to gather my wits."

Elizabeth nodded and descended the staircase for the drawing room.

Aunt Prudence slept in the chair beside the hearth. A low fire burned in the grate, and Elizabeth could see the perspiration beading her great-aunt's brow.

Taking care not to wake the old woman, Elizabeth lifted an empty goblet from Aunt Prudence's hand, then slipped the woolen shawl from her shoulders.

Elizabeth dutifully folded the shawl and placed it on the settee, then carefully, so as not to wrinkle her gown, sat down to wait.

Several minutes passed, and Aunt Prudence's heavy breathing was making Elizabeth sleepy. She rose and walked to the mantelpiece. Lifting her father's keeping box from the shelf, she unlocked it. Quietly Elizabeth withdrew her father's *Book of Maladies and Remedies* and removed from it the marriage register signed by the Prince of Wales and Maria Fitzherbert. Might they truly be her parents?

How amazing it was that the register had been hidden inside this very book for nearly their whole lives, and they had never known it.

She set the register on the tea table and ran her fingertip along the edge Lotharian had cut. *How utterly amazing*. With the tip of her tongue poised on the center of her top lip, she dug her fingers inside the pocket the glued pages had created. She glanced across at the damnable register again.

She wished she had been the one to pull the register from the book—rather than Anne. She knew her sister felt a special guilt for being the one to free the register from its hiding place.

If she could reverse time, Elizabeth decided that she would have claimed the right, and the guilt, to discover the register inside the book.

Just then, an unopened edge broke open from the press of her absently probing fingers. "Oh, perdition!" She gasped at the volume of own expletive and looked at once at Aunt Prudence to be sure she had not heard her. The elderly woman stirred momentarily, but then her slow, steady breathing resumed.

Elizabeth released her own breath and looked down at the half-opened page. There was writing, not printed text inside the created pocket. She glanced up at Aunt Prudence. Still asleep.

Carefully she eased opened the last glued edge of the two pages and separated them. There, pasted on the inner front page, was a small, square missive, written on paper almost as thin as gossamer.

When the moon crests the bridge crossing the Serpentine this night, I will wait, MacLaren. No favor you ask of Her is too great. Your confidence in this matter is requisite.

Frances, Countess of Jersey

Elizabeth held the book closer to her eyes. *No, it cannot be.* But the missive was hidden along with the register. Lady Jersey?

She snatched up the vellum from the table and stared at the missive and the folded page from the marriage register. Lady Jersey wanted this.

A shiver spread over Elizabeth's skin. She needed no other proof of the validity of her bloodline than this knowledge.

She heard a mournful sob and the sound of footfalls on the stair treads. She set the book and the register on the tea table and started for the doorway, intent on telling Anne what she'd found. When Elizabeth heard her sister crying softly, she stopped short.

She turned back around, to hide the book away again, when she saw Aunt Prudence swaying unsteadily before the fire hearth, the register in her hand.

Her heart pounded in her chest. Aunt Prudence looked up at her, appearing confused. Elizabeth nodded. "Do it," she whispered. "*Now.*"

Almack's

It was only eight of the clock, and already the *on-dit* columnists were calling Lady MacLaren's betrothal ball for her son a rousing success despite the fact that so many young men of Quality were still at the Continent. It mattered not to the columnists, it seemed, that fully half the guests had not managed to set slipper inside Almack's yet.

Already carriages stood three deep outside the assembly room doors, with a mile behind those waiting to decant their passengers at the most anticipated event of the season.

Anne and Elizabeth, who rode with Lady Upperton in her carriage, were about a mile away in the carriage line. It was just as well. Any time spent waiting outside Almack's was another clutch of minutes during which Anne could convince herself that she would not have to cry off before all of London society.

She hadn't even seen Laird, thanks to interference by the Old Rakes and Lady Upperton, who had vowed to make this night as painless as possible for Anne.

But she knew that they could not protect Laird from what was coming. No doubt he expected the night of his life, dancing with Anne, without a care in his world.

And only two weeks before, that blissful life might have been theirs. But no longer.

Much to Lady MacLaren's dismay, Anne politely declined a ride to the ball in Lord MacLaren's carriage. Lady Upperton tried to explain her reasoning to the countess, blaming it on Anne's nerves, for now that the couple had returned to London, stories of Lord MacLaren's heroism had swept through Town like a wild fire.

Everyone wished to glimpse the simple Cornwall miss who'd fallen off a bridge—and then a cliff, and caught the heart of a newly belted earl.

Anne and Elizabeth could not walk to the Bond Street shops without being followed by debutantes asking for secrets on how to engage an earl.

It had gotten so the two never went outside without costuming themselves as scullery maids, but that didn't last very long, either. Merchants in the ribbon and millinery shops they most enjoyed frequenting were not always willing to wait on customers who didn't appear to have enough money to spend.

The *Times* was littered with stories of young misses leaping from the bridge over the Serpentine, hoping a hero would appear, pluck her from the watery depths, and then marry her.

There had even been a report about a matron pushing her daughter into the water when a certain Viscount Apsley was out riding in Hyde Park.

So far, however, there had been no reports of injuries, rescues or . . . marriages, for that matter.

Anne only hoped that after she did what she must to protect Laird, even if that meant breaking his heart tonight, the ridiculous Serpentine-jumping craze might cease for good.

Then perhaps Anne, the invisible, could return to her blissfully dull life once more.

"Have you seen Miss Anne yet?" Apsley studied the tailoring of Laird's coat for indications of superiority. He claimed he was still slightly miffed that they were both wearing a bottle-green cutaway coat, Laird's of kerseymere and Arthur's of camlet. But he was pleased, at least, that they shared the same excellent taste in clothing.

Laird shifted from one foot to the other, at the top of the grand staircase, as he surveyed the herd of patrons filing into Almack's for the betrothal ball. "Haven't seen her."

"You know who I did see, though only from a distance, so I could be entirely wrong—Lady Henceforth!"

Laird grabbed Apsley's shoulders.

"Have a care, man; don't want to wrinkle the

coat before the ladies have had a chance to see it."

"Are you certain it was Constance you saw?" Laird gave Apsley a little shake.

"No, no, I told you I *wasn't* sure. Why would she come here anyway? I sincerely doubt your mother included Lady Henceforth on her guest list."

"I'm sorry. It's just that before I left St. Albans, Anne found an old letter that had never been delivered to me."

"Old love letter, from Lady Henceforth, was it?"

"Actually it was from Graham. I don't know why he never sent it to me." Laird took Apsley's arm and drew him in an alcove so they could speak more privately. "The letter explained his reason for joining the military when a war was raging."

"I always thought he was a heroic sort, the dutiful son, that sort of thing."

"As did I, so when my father announced that Graham had run off to fight for England, something he claimed I was too cowardly to do, I believed just that. And then, when my brother was killed . . ."

"You believed you were to blame."

Laird nodded his head. "And brandy became my best mate—no offense, Apsley."

"None taken. She's good a friend of mine as well." Apsley grinned good-naturedly. "So what did the bleedin' letter say?"

"Not at all what I expected. It seems that Graham and Constance, Lady Henceforth, were deeply in love. But when he offered for her, nearly three years ago, her parents turned him away. He was the spare, not the heir, and they had already had a more promising offer from Lord Henceforth."

"I've been meaning to ask you about that. Did they just prop Henceforth up for the wedding ceremony, or was he still alive?" Apsley grinned, but his smile fell away when Laird did not join in his amusement. "All I am saying is that the man must have been eighty years if he was a day."

"Yes, he was old. But he was married to Constance. From the letter, I have gathered that this pained Graham so greatly that he purchased a commission to put as much distance as he could between the new Lady Henceforth and himself."

"Graham's death was not your fault." Apsley

clapped Laird on the back. "You know that for certain now, don't you?"

Laird bit his lower lip as he nodded his head. "I do. Gads, you can imagine my relief. The guilt had been almost too much to bear. Graham was not only my brother, he was my friend."

"Old Henceforth died right after the wedding, didn't he?" Apsley asked, his gaze flitting around for a wine-bearing footman.

"Yes. And after her mourning, Constance leaned on my shoulder. I leaned on hers, too—Graham had been missing for two months, but I still held out weak hope that he lived. And Christ, she was vulnerable and beautiful . . ."

"I suppose a marriage between the two of you might have worked."

Laird huffed at that comment. "If she hadn't been so repulsed by me when she heard about my black reputation. Sickened enough to cry off—or so she claimed." Laird shook his head. "Turns out, the truth of the matter was that when Graham's division reappeared from their mission, he sent her a letter asking her to marry him when he returned home."

"And so Lady Henceforth cried off. But Graham never did come home."

"No, he didn't," Laird intoned softly.

Apsley wrinkled his brow, and the two did not speak a word for several long moments. "This night belongs to you and to Anne. Not the past. It is time to celebrate your future!"

"You've got it exactly right." Laird felt his entire being lighten. "Come on, maybe Anne is in the ballroom with the countess."

Anne and Elizabeth stood with Lady Upperton and the Old Rakes near the orchestra dais in the grand ballroom.

"Are you sure you want to do this?" Elizabeth asked her.

"I am sure I do *not* want to do this. I love him, and want nothing more than to spend my life together with Laird, but I will not involve him in possible treason." Anne's eyes began to sting. "Oh, drat. I am going to cry again."

"But Anne, I must tell you something—" Elizabeth began.

"Dear, you do not have to cry off just to protect him," Lady Upperton interrupted. Plucking her own lace handkerchief from inside her sleeve, she dabbed the tears from Anne's face. "You just have to hold the secret to your heart . . . forever."

"What secret is that, Miss Royle?" a feminine voice asked in dulcet tones.

Anne whirled around to see Lady Henceforth, a swatch of lace affixed somehow to her thin nose bandage for the occasion. "How did you . . . I mean, I had not expected to see you here this evening, Lady Henceforth."

"Really?" Lady Henceforth smiled coolly. "I wanted to see it for myself."

"See what? Anne's first dance with Lord MacLaren?" Elizabeth sniped. She turned back to her sister. "Please, Anne, come with me. I must tell you something *important*."

Lady Henceforth pushed her way between the sisters. "Oh no. That will not be so nearly as diverting as the moment Anne cries off and leaves Lord MacLaren standing alone . . . again." Lady Henceforth flicked her dark slash of an eyebrow. "Apsley let it slip one night, after a few too many glasses of brandy. This betrothal is a farce—a wager—and nothing more."

Laird suddenly appeared at Anne's side. "Are you so sure of that, Constance?"

"It was a lie from the beginning. Like all of Miss Royle's other tall tales of heroism. She actually has a wonderful sense of imagination. You know, I even think she might have convinced herself that she loves you."

"I do love him." Anne moved slowly toward Lady Henceforth and peered down at her. "I think you should leave, Lady Henceforth."

"Oh, I shall." She stepped backward, knocking Elizabeth deep into a gathering crowd. "In a moment. As soon as I expose the lie of your betrothal."

"Why would you do this?" Anne asked. "I have never shown you anything but kindness."

"Until you gave Laird that letter from Graham . . . making me out to be not much more than a lightskirt." Her nostrils flared in anger. "After MacLaren came back to St. Albans with you, I saw that he had changed. I marveled at the improvement. So, then when Apsley told me about the wager, I realized that I had been given a second chance. Marrying Laird would no longer be a stain upon my name. It would be an honor."

"The point of my showing you Graham's letter, Constance," Laird explained gently, "was that my brother loved you in a way that I never could. We were not meant to be together, despite what I had believed just days before. Graham's letter proved that to me."

Lady Henceforth's eyes grew large. "Are you saying that you would truly choose a habitual liar from Cornwall over me?"

"I am." Laird placed Anne's hand on his forearm. "Look there, Anne, the dancers are taking their places on the floor. Let us join them."

Anne's eyes glistened as she gazed up at the man she loved. How she wished she did not have to cry off. That she could share a life with Laird as perfect as the one her sister Mary and her husband, the Duke of Blackstone, now shared. At least, she consoled herself, she could pretend . . . until the end of the dance set.

Anne and Laird stepped onto the floor, to a round of thunderous applause. Lady MacLaren stood beside the orchestra conductor, beaming with pride and happiness.

But then Lady Henceforth rushed into the center of the dancers. Tears of humiliation filled her brown eyes. "What a lark! What a lark, indeed," she cried out, until the room grew still and silent. "I have just learned that our Lord MacLaren here and Miss Anne Royle are playing a grand joke on us all."

Confused murmurs rolled through the expansive ball room.

"Yes, it's true!" She walked in a large circle so that everyone could see and hear what she was about to say.

"Why, imagine my surprise when I learned that they are not betrothed at all!"

Chatter erupted in every corner of the room. Young women gasped, matrons swooned, and gentlemen chuckled and paid off their bets right there on the dance floor.

Anne, her eyes brimming with unshed tears, squeezed Laird's hand. "I'm sorry, Laird, but I must do this . . . for you." She turned and walked alone to the center of the dance floor.

"No, Anne—" Elizabeth's voice pierced Anne's focus. She could just see her sister, fighting her way back through the seemingly endless rings of onlookers circling the floor. "Stop! Please, Anne. Do not say it!"

Anne looked away. She had to do it. Had to do it now before she lost her resolve. "Lady Henceforth is right!" Anne breathed deeply as the crowd quieted. She faced Laird, holding his gaze for several precious seconds before she said what she must. "The Earl of MacLaren and I are not betrothed."

"No!" Elizabeth cried. "Anne, *no!*"

The crowd roared, sending every bone in Anne's body shaking. She closed her eyes for a moment to prepare for the final blow. When she finally opened them, Laird was standing at her side.

He took her hand in his and touched it to his lips. "Anne, I love *you*, and only you," he whispered in her ear. "So please, allow me the honor."

Lifting his other hand in the air, he signaled for silence.

Anne looked at him in utter confusion. What was he about to do?

"We are no longer betrothed. Yes, yes, it's true." Laird faced Anne, holding both of her hands now. "Because we are . . . *already married*."

A jolt shot through Anne, and for a moment she was certain her eyes would pop from their sockets.

He was lying. Lying to everyone!

The ballroom erupted into wild applause. Lady MacLaren signaled the orchestra to resume, and Laird swept Anne into his arms.

Tears streamed down her cheeks.

God, she loved him, but she couldn't allow him to be connected with her. "Laird, please listen to me," she began.

"After the dance, my love." Laird was beaming with happiness.

"No, I must—"

Elizabeth reached her then. She grabbed Anne's shoulders and spun her from Laird's embrace. "Stop now, Anne, and listen to what I am telling you. You do *not* have to do this."

"Yes, I do, Elizabeth." Anne tried to turn again to face Laird.

Elizabeth yanked her back. "No you don't. I burned it, Anne. There is no proof. Do you understand me? You do not need to cry off to protect him."

A cool sweat broke over Anne's skin. "What are you saying?"

"The register no longer exists." Elizabeth smiled. "It's gone. I burned it."

"Burned it? But, Elizabeth, the register is all we had to prove—"

"No proof, no matter what it might have meant to us or even the Crown, is worth seeing my sister's heart broken."

"But Elizabeth, what you did is—"

"Something we shall not speak of again." Elizabeth kissed Anne's cheek and grinned. "Now go. Your *husband* is waiting."

Anne slowly turned around and gazed up at Laird's handsome lying face. God, how she loved him.

"Shall we dance, my darling?" He offered his hand to her, and when she took it, drew her close enough to share a secret wink. "After all," he told her in a tone loud enough for anyone nearby to hear, "it will be our first—*as husband and wife*."

Berkeley Square
The next evening

"Hear, hear!" Elizabeth cheered.

Everyone raised his glass into the air, toasting the not-so-newly-betrothed Anne and Laird, Earl of MacLaren. Everyone except Aunt Prudence, who slept, snoring softly, in the hearthside chair.

And Lilywhite.

Sir Lumley just could not bring himself to toast the joyous couple. Not until he had confessed the secret he'd held inside all these long years. And that confession was not going to be easy.

"What is it, Sir Lumley? Are you not pleased

that your charge and I are engaged?" Laird flicked his eyebrow upward, though a smile still lingered on his lips. Lilywhite hoped MacLaren's good spirits would linger, too—after he made his confession.

"I-I . . ." Sir Lumley's puffy cheeks felt as heated and red as the setting sun. "MacLaren, I must admit something to you. To you, too, Anne and Elizabeth. I cannot allow you, MacLaren, to continue believing that your father was entirely selfish, for indeed he was not. He was my dear friend for many years, until one night when I was too deep in my cups to know enough to curb my words."

Laird looked to Anne, as if expecting her to explain what Lilywhite meant by his words, but she was as lost in the shadows about this as he was.

"Go on, Lilywhite." Lotharian flicked his hand. "Tell them. This is long overdue, if you ask me."

Lilywhite lowered his gaze and bobbed his chin upon his chest. "I can't deny it." He looked up at Anne and Elizabeth, and then turned his eyes fixedly upon Laird. "Everyone, Whig and Tory, believed that either Charles Fox or your father, MacLaren, had somehow come into possession of the marriage register signed by both the Prince of Wales and Maria Fitzherbert."

"Yes, yes, we know this." Elizabeth wrung her hands impatiently.

"But a few of us in the prince's inner circle, heard, too, that Lady Jersey petitioned MacLaren to surrender the register to her . . . on behalf of the queen." Sir Lumley glanced around the room. Every person was poised on his last word. "Well, this would make good sense to MacLaren. The king was ailing and needed to secure the royal lineage. If the queen could persuade Prinny to set aside the notion of declaring his illegal marriage to Maria Fitzherbert to the people, passage of a bill to make him regent would be much more likely. And if the queen thought possessing the wedding register, the only true proof of this marriage would make her son regent, then he should deliver it to her."

"You appear confused, Elizabeth," Gallantine said. "Let me try to explain this. MacLaren's only reason for concealing the register was to prevent William Pitt from presenting it as proof of an illegal marriage to a Catholic in an attempt to discredit the prince. The register had to remain hidden to prevent public opinion from turning against the prince before he could be named regent. MacLaren knew the queen could be trusted to sequester the register—and, too, that she would be forever indebted to him for seeing it into her hands."

"And so he gave it to her?" Anne shook her head. "How, then, did my father obtain the register?"

"Because of me." Lilywhite sighed. "And I risked your very lives in the process."

Anne and Elizabeth exchanged concerned glances.

"I started to say earlier, I was foxed one night. I had heard rumors that MacLaren was considering delivering the register to Lady Jersey. But I knew he shouldn't trust her. She was cunning. She was the prince's latest mistress. And, according to Royle, she and the queen had sought to see Maria Fitzherbert's triplets dead. I told MacLaren everything."

"What did he do?" Laird slowly came to his feet.

"He didn't *seem* to do anything. We stopped hearing rumors about the register. It was as though it had simply disappeared." Lilywhite raised his hands to Laird. "Royle and MacLaren had once been friends. We all had. It's very clear what happened to the register. Don't you see?"

"No," Anne said. "I don't."

Lilywhite huffed a frustrated sigh from his huge middle. "Royle had the register. MacLaren had the page cutter with the location of the register etched upon it."

"MacLaren gave our father the register—to help prove who we are." Elizabeth's eyes were like globes. "Lord MacLaren, your father could have used the register to gain favor with the Crown . . . to further his position within the House of Lords, but he didn't."

Lotharian cast a quick, yet decidedly derisive glance at Sir Lumley. "If anyone else had overheard Lilywhite's drunken conversation with MacLaren in Boodle's that night"—he sighed and settled his bony hand on Laird's shoulder— "and it was discovered that Royle, the prince's own physician, had saved Maria Fitzherbert's babies, the girls' lives might have been in imminent danger."

Lady Upperton raised her finger and took over the conversation, as was her habit. "Yes, grave danger—if no evidence existed to help support the claim that the gels were of royal blood. Oh, the marriage register mightn't have been much in the way of proof, but it may have been just enough to spare their lives. I fear we may never know."

Laird turned to Anne and lifted her hands in his. "My father—"

Anne stared up at him in disbelief as she finished his thought. "Might have saved *my* life."

Laird's breath caught the very moment he comprehended the underlying meaning of her words. He stared blankly at Anne for several seconds, and then the skin at the outer edges of his eyes crinkled upward. He smiled, and Anne knew Laird had glimpsed another side of his father, the man his mother had loved so much.

"His sacrificing the register might have saved my life, too," Elizabeth blurted. Suddenly she spun around and squinted fretfully at the coal fire smoldering in the hearth. "Gorblimey, I hope we don't need the register . . . *anymore*."

Everyone laughed politely at Elizabeth's slightly inappropriate comment, except, Anne was quick to notice, Lord Lotharian, who tipped his glass to his lips and sipped his brandy as he peered pensively over its rim at Elizabeth.

Chapter 21

How to Engage an Earl

And so they were married—a full week after their glittering nuptials had been reported by every *on dit* columnist in London.

It was amazing, especially to Elizabeth, how eerily accurate the newspapers' descriptions had been in predicting a future event. Had the date of the reported wedding not been off by a sennight, she might have wondered if someone sitting in the box pews, or in the galleries above, had taken detailed notes.

For indeed, just as the newspaper columnists had reported, Laird Allan, Earl of MacLaren, had obtained a special license and had engaged Robert Hodgson himself, the rector of St. George's, to perform the brief but poignant marriage service.

By the flickering light of dozens of beeswax

candles (for the marriage was conducted secretly), Hodgson joined a most joyous Miss Anne Royle with the newly belted Earl of MacLaren, proclaiming them man and wife before God, country, three Old Rakes, two ladies of society, a sleeping elderly great-aunt, a viscount, and one miss, late of Cornwall but currently residing in Berkeley Square.

Though the wedding was not the magnificent society event the new Dowager MacLaren had once considered necessary for her son and a family of such high standing in society, it was everything she had dreamed it would be.

Laird was happy at last and in love, and what more could a mother ever hope for her son?

Late that same evening, Apsley took home one of the George Romney canvas lovelies from Laird's town house wall—even though he agreed he didn't really deserve it, due to the fact that the wager had not been properly listed in the book at White's.

But it didn't really matter.

What did matter was that Lotharian, as always, won *his* wager. Miss Anne Royle had married the Earl of MacLaren—the very man he had selected for her. Oh, maneuvering this gel to the altar had been slightly more difficult than ushering her sister Mary down the aisle of St. George's, but in the end, he'd done it.

As they left the MacLarens' town house on Cockspur Street, Gallantine and Lilywhite handed over heavy leather pouches of gold to the victor.

"Someday, Lotharian, your age will get the better of you and you will fail in your complex matchmaking machinations," Lilywhite muttered as they staggered out to their waiting carriage.

"Oh, I don't know about that, old man." Lotharian grinned. "I have a few good years left in me—and one more Royle sister to see matched."

"You might have had us all caught up in this scheme, but three for three? Surely the Royle sisters are on to your game by now. I know we are, and I do not think you can manage it again," Gallantine announced.

"Care to wager on that, gentlemen?" Lotharian cast a wink at Lady Upperton, who knew the groundwork for Elizabeth's match was, at that very moment, moving into place.

She winked back at him, then flipped open her cutwork fan to conceal a grin and her complicity.

As the last guests, the Old Rakes and Lady Upperton, departed the celebration, Anne and Laird raised their goblets in the air and privately toasted their love.

"Would you have believed me if I told you I loved you the moment you stole my goblet from me in the drawing room?" Laird leaned close and nuzzled the soft place behind Anne's ear.

"My husband, the rake. Promise me you will never change." Anne grabbed the back of his neck and dragged his mouth to hers.

Her distraction worked, and without him being the wiser, she lifted his goblet with the fingertips of her free hand.

As they broke their kiss, she laughed softly and sipped from her glass and then the one she'd stolen from him.

"As long as you promise me you will never change, either." Laird leaned in and kissed her lips gently. "I love you, Lady MacLaren."

Anne smiled, even as his lips lowered over hers again. "And I love you, *my Laird*."

"My, I am feeling oh so exhausted." As Laird started for the passageway, he glanced over his shoulder at Anne. A mischievous grin tilted his lips.

"Where are you going, Lord MacLaren?" Anne stood in the middle of the drawing room with a filled goblet in each hand.

"Oh, lass." He tossed a wink at her. "The moon is full and bright this eve. I think you'll know where to find me."

Epilogue

The crescent moon, perched high in the starry sky, was too dim to light Festidious's way to Hyde Park. It was not such a long walk, but the butler trembled nonetheless, unaccustomed to journeying anywhere at night beyond the glow of the gaslights lining Pall Mall.

He had not thought to wear his boots, and now feared that the damp earth of Rotten Row, giving beneath his feet with each slow step, would ruin his slippers beyond service. Still, he trudged along until he reached the place the lady had designated—the bridge crossing the Serpentine.

Festidious did not see the figure garbed in ebony, standing at the center of the bridge, until he was very nearly upon her.

A thrill shot through his middle. This was

all so beyond him. So daring. But he was loyal, above all, and knew his duty.

"Do you have them?" she asked softly.

"I do, my lady." Festidious's hand was shaking as he handed her the small leather portfolio containing the purloined bundle of correspondence.

"You told no one that you located the letters?" She raised the lace hem of her veil and peered up at him with those piercing eyes of hers.

"No one, my lady. I swear it. I was alone when I discovered them. They were exactly where you said they would be."

"Very good." She lowered her veil, tipped her head in thanks, and had just started to turn to leave, when she paused. "Will you escort me to my carriage?"

Festidious beamed with pride as he offered her his arm. "Of course, my lady. Anything."

She read them all that very night, dropping them as she finished, one by one, into the flames of the hearth; watching them glow red and curl before blackening to worthless ash.

All except one—the single letter that truly mattered.

Holding the letter to the golden illumination of a single candle, she read its text from beginning to end once more.

She smiled to herself, extraordinarily pleased with her own ingenuity, then folded it most carefully and gently settled it inside the box.

Turning the brass key in the escutcheon, she locked away the dangerous letter the Royle sisters searched for . . . but now would never find.

Unless *she* wished it.

And she had not yet decided whether she did.

Author's Note

I love to find gaps in history, tiny cracks between the recorded known and the unknown, where I can jump in and play the favorite game of authors everywhere—*what if?*

How to Engage an Earl, for instance, explores yet another unknown in Regency-era history. Maria Fitzherbert, a Catholic widow, and the Prince of Wales were married secretly. At this time, not only was such a union illegal, but public knowledge of Prinny's marriage to a Catholic could greatly jeopardize his chances of being named Regent. The Tories, led by William Pitt, the Prime Minister, opposed rule being transferred from the ailing king to the Prince of Wales, and did everything in their power to prevent it. At one time, the Tories were even rumored to have obtained the couple's signed wedding register page (proof positive of the illegal marriage) with the intent of using it against the Prince of Wales. Suddenly the register disappeared. Who took the register? What happened to it? *Jump.* Well, I knew who stole it and why.

Other times, my characters jump (in this story, quite literally), and a little artistic license is needed on my part to bridge the gap beween fiction and historical accuracy. For example, for story reasons I created a span across the sparkling Serpentine dividing it from the Long Water, since George Rennie's bridge would not be built until 1826.

There is no question that breaches in history have provided inspiration for *How to Seduce a Duke*, the first story in the Royle sisters trilogy, as well as *How to Engage an Earl.* Be sure to look for *How to Propose to a Prince* next spring for the answer to the biggest historical "what if" of the series—are the Royle sisters the secret daughters of the Prince of Wales and Maria Fitzherbert? Stay tuned.

Katheryn Caskie

*The scandalous adventures of the
Royle sisters continue in
Kathryn Caskie's next unforgettable
Avon Treasure*
HOW TO PROPOSE TO A PRINCE
Available Spring 2008

A Royle Wedding

It was raining . . . a bit.

Only a bit, her sister had said.

Elizabeth Royle looked down at the embroidered skirt of her jacconet muslin frock, and became instantly nauseated.

She and Anne had been walking for only two minutes, and already she was soaked to her knees. The umbrella they shared had done nothing to protect her dress or azure crepe mantle from the white sheets of rain sweeping down Pall Mall.

Her Bourbon walking ensemble would never be the same. Ever.

Had her sister Anne not been leaving for her honeymoon in Brighton on the morrow, Elizabeth would have never agreed to shop with her for a few sartorial essentials on such a horrid day as this.

At least it had afforded her the opportunity, before Anne left on her journey, to begin to tell her sister about the man she intended to marry.

"Oh heavens, Elizabeth, that means nothing. It was just a dream," Anne said.

"No it wasn't. It was more." Elizabeth stopped abruptly, causing an annoyed couple to unexpectedly veer off the damp pavers into the squishing mud edging the street. She shoved a loose copper lock that dangled before her eye beneath her Bourbon hat and over her ear. "I swear to you, Anne, last night I wrapped a sliver of your wedding cake and put it under my pillow, exactly as Mrs. Polkshank had advised, and it worked—I dreamed of *him*, the man I would marry."

Frustrated, Anne peeled a mist-dampened lock of golden hair from her brow, then grabbed her sister's arm and started her down Pall Mall again. "And he was a . . . *prince?*"

Heated surged into Elizabeth's cheeks. "Well . . . yes."

"Do you not see how preposterous this notion is? How are you so sure he is a prince? What did you see in your dream? And, I must remind you, it was just a dream." Anne raised a cynical eyebrow at her as they walked.

"I-I did not see anything to indicate his royal standing. I just . . . felt it," Elizabeth tried to explain.

"What *did* you see, then? It is possible you are misinterpreting what you saw." Anne obviously noted Elizabeth's embarrassment and sought to placate her.

"That he is ruggedly handsome, though there is an air of controlled strength about him. I could see it in the purposeful way he moved. The way others moved about him, deferred to him."

"What about his hair, his face? Has he got a long nose, or a weak chin—some feature that might help you identify him in a crowd?" Anne grinned.

"His face is beautiful. Perfect." She scowled at Anne. "And I would recognize him anywhere. His eyes are so unusual. They are as leaden gray as this sky, but a thin ring of summer blue surrounds them. I have never seen eyes like that—except in my dream." Elizabeth drifted off, lost in the memory of those haunting eyes. Instinctively she turned to the sound of a team of horses clopping past, but in the rain and the thick fog rising up from the street, she could see nothing but a huge shadow slowly passing them by.

"Elizabeth! Keep walking. We're nearly to the draper's shop." Anne squeezed Elizabeth's arm and urged her along, chattering as they walked. "Tell me more about your gentleman."

"His hair is thick, dark, and wavy, and his skin is almost golden, as though he'd spent a goodly amount of time out of doors."

"Well, it's clear then." Anne laughed mockingly. "You are to marry a farmer. Oh dear. Your guardian won't much like that. Gallantine and his cronies will accept nothing less than a peer of the realm for the secret daughter of the Prince of Wales." She feigned a mournful sigh. "But . . . if you dreamed of marrying a farmer, I suppose it must be true." Anne teased, earning her arm a hard pinch from Elizabeth.

"Please do not tease me about this. And I told you, he is a prince. My dreams *do* come true frequently, so I am not taking this premonition lightly."

"Oh, it's a premonition now, is it?" Anne chuckled, obviously not understanding how vivid this presentiment had been to Elizabeth. "Lizzie, your dreams do come true, but only some of the time. And even then, you usually get half of what you see *wrong*. You'd do as well

332

flipping a tuppence to determine your future."

"Well, continue to doubt me if you must. But won't you be a plucked goose when an offer is made and I marry before the summer ends."

"Before the summer ... *this* summer? Oh, Elizabeth, you haven't even met your husband-to-be yet. There is no possible way you will find a ring on your finger in just two months."

"Why not? You did, and Mary as well, and now she and the duke are about to have a baby."

"Oh sweeting, please do not set your heart on this course. You will only be disappointed."

Elizabeth suddenly stopped, yanking her sister to a halt along with her. "*Gorblimey*. Anne, it's ... him. Right *there*."

She poked a shaking finger in the direction of a fog-cloaked gentleman stepping down from the grandest carriage she had ever seen.

But he looked even finer than the gilt carriage. On the shoulders of his kerseymere coat were braided gold epaulets, and a red satin sash swept across his broad chest to his lean hip. Several military medals were pinned to his chest. Two regimental-straight lines of gleaming buttons, too brilliant to be mere brass, ran down his dark blue coat.

"What? That nobleman?" Anne blinked at him, clearly disbelieving that this man was the *one* Elizabeth would marry. "Well, his skin is rather sun-kissed, I'll give you that, but he is certainly not a farmer."

Elizabeth glowered at Anne. "*You* said he was a farmer, not I!" When she turned to peer at him again, he was gone. "Oh, lud, we've lost him."

"No, we haven't." Anne inclined her head to the shop just four doors down Pall Mall. "He went into Hamilton and Company, just there."

Elizabeth widened her eyes to see through the fog and rain, and managed to glimpse two liveried footmen entering a shop.

"Ah, jeweler to the Crown by Royal Appointment. He is definitely *not* a farmer."

Elizabeth paid her sister's ribbing no mind. She hastened her step, hauling Anne along with her. "Mayhap he has gone inside to choose a ring for me." She winked at her sister. "Have you considered that, Anne?"

Elizabeth paused before the shop door. A steady stream of water poured from the Hamilton and Company sign above, pounding the umbrella she and Anne huddled beneath like a roaring waterfall.

Anne tugged at her arm. "Elizabeth, we are being drenched. Why do you delay? He is right inside. Come along."

Elizabeth trembled. If her premonition was true, her future lay just beyond, and yet she could not seem to step over the threshold. What if, as Anne claimed, it was only a dream—a vision she had only half right?

Before she could worry over it a moment longer, her sister pressed down the brass latch, and the shop door opened. A bell sounded overhead as Anne dragged her through the door, noisily heralding their entrance to the startled shopkeeper.

The dark-haired gentleman they had pursued whirled around as well. His gray eyes locked with Elizabeth's.

Anne leaned close and whispered. "Pity, it's a diamond and ruby brooch he's considering, Lizzie, not a ring for you."

Elizabeth didn't say a word. She could not. It was *he*.

Her prince.

The shopkeeper smiled up at Anne. "Good afternoon, Lady MacLaren, Miss Royle."

"Good afternoon, sir," Anne replied. "I see you

are occupied, but worry not. My sister and I are in no hurry to be served. In truth, we would be most content browsing your cases and shelves."

"Absolutely, Lady MacLaren." The shop-keeper bobbed a quick bow. "But I shall have my son attend to your needs presently."

Elizabeth wrenched her gaze from the gentleman and focused on a case of baubles and rare gems, but she could feel the heat of his eyes still upon her.

"Come, Elizabeth. Look at these *tiaras*. Stunning, simply stunning."

Tiaras? Her cheeks were blazing now, and she hurried to catch up to her sister, who had wandered across the deep, narrow shop. "Cease these games at once, Anne," Elizabeth whispered hotly. "You are not the least amusing, and your antics are embarrassing me."

"I am only jesting, Lizzie." Anne grinned up at her, but when her gaze met Elizabeth's fretful eyes, she realized her unease. "I apologize. Really, I do. Though . . . these tiaras are lovely, aren't they?" She turned and glanced over her shoulder momentarily. "Is it him?"

Elizabeth sucked her lips into her mouth and gave her head a nod.

"Are you sure?"

"*Yes.*" She clasped her sister's wrist and drew her closer. "Oh God. What shall I do?"

Anne glanced at the gentleman again, and Elizabeth hesitantly followed her gaze. Now he was examining a necklace dripping with graduated droplets of verdant emeralds and snowy pearls.

"First, remove your wilted hat." Anne whisked the soggy Bourbon hat, with its dripping white feather, from Elizabeth's head and shoved it under her own arm.

"Anne, you're crushing my hat," Elizabeth ground out between her teeth.

Anne didn't reply. Her eyes shot in the handsome gentleman's direction again, then she quickly plucked four hairpins from Elizabeth's hair, sending a cascade of red curls tumbling down her back.

Before Elizabeth could protest, Anne had shoved her fingers through the hat-matted hair at her crown to restore the fullness of her curly hair. "Well now, much better. You want to present well, do you not?"

A twittering male voice suddenly called out from the rear of the shop, "Lady MacLaren, Miss Royle."

Startled by the intrusion, Elizabeth snapped her head around to see a young man in close-fitting blue coat and tighter still gray pantaloons, hurrying toward them, waving his hands excitedly in the air.

Elizabeth angled her head toward her sister. "How do the shopkeepers know our names?"

"They probably read them in the *Times*," replied a rich, resonant male voice coming from directly behind her.

Elizabeth's eyes widened. *Oh dear.* She knew who was standing there, so close that she could feel the heat radiating from his body.

Anne covertly sank an elbow into Elizabeth's side. "Turn around."

Slowly, Elizabeth swiveled her head in his direction, following its momentum with her body a scant second later, until she faced him fully and met his piercing gaze. She could not help but stare.

Lud, from such close proximity she could see . . . a ring of clear blue edging the silvery gray of his eyes. She gasped. Any doubt as to his identity evaporated in that instant.

This man standing before her was plucked directly from her dream. He was the gentleman she would one day marry.

Anne whirled about, having heard Elizabeth's surprised reaction to the man. She blinked when she discerned the unusual color of his eyes— exactly as Elizabeth had described. Anne clapped a hand to her chest. "I-I beg your pardon, sir, it seems neither of us had been aware of your approach."

"I do apologize, Lady MacLaren. I did not mean to startle you . . . or Miss Royle." He exhaled a staggered breath as though somewhat embarrassed. "Miss Royle had asked . . . and, well, I only meant to explain to her that your wedding, Lady MacLaren, was reported in the *Times*."

"And every other newspaper in the realm," the young shop clerk blurted. "I saw at least four caricatures of you both. It would be hard to mistake your faces. Why, Lady MacLaren, your betrothal ball at Almack's is still the talk of London."

"Bertrum!" Mr. Hamilton hissed.

The young shop clerk, realizing he had forgotten his place, turned on his heel and started for the back of the shop, when Elizabeth's would-be fiancé unexpectedly called out, "Young man."

Bertrum, the clerk, stopped and turned to face

them, his head hanging low. "I beg your forgiveness, Your Royal Highness."

Elizabeth gasped again and looked immediately to Anne, whose golden eyes had gone wide.

"Your Royal Highness? No, no, you mistake me for another." A ruddiness swept the gentleman's cheekbones. He straightened his back, and his chest expanded as he prepared to address the women. "Please excuse me, Lady MacLaren, Miss Royle. When I approached, I had only wished to request a small favor. I should not have even thought it, or spoken to you, but now that I have, I am duty-compelled to properly introduce myself. I am Lord Whitevale." He bowed deeply. "I hope you will forgive my earlier impertinence."

From the periphery of her vision, Elizabeth saw the clerk roll his eyes disbelievingly. Odd behavior . . .

Within the next moments, Anne had politely introduced them both. "My lord, what favor did you wish to ask of us? Of course we shall assist you if possible."

"I-I . . ." He gestured for the clerk. "That tiara there. The one the ladies were viewing."

Young Hamilton reached into the jewel case and lifted a glittering diamond tiara from a tuft of black velvet. "This one, my lord?"

"Yes." He took the jewel-encrusted tiara from the clerk, and then held it out to Elizabeth. "Might you wear this for me, for just a moment. Please."

Elizabeth forced a polite smile and nodded. She reached for the tiara, but Lord Whitevale suddenly waved her hand away.

"Would you allow me, Miss Royle?" he asked.

Once more, Elizabeth nodded mutely. Her hands were trembling so fiercely that she probably would not be able to position the tiara upon her head properly anyway.

She did not say a word, la, she barely breathed, for fear she would shriek with excitement as he raised the weighty tiara and eased it into the curls of her hair as he settled it atop her head.

Her dream was coming true. She knew it! Well, half true at least. So Lord Whitevale was not a prince. But that was of no consequence. Here she stood with a sparkling diamond tiara on her head, placed there by the man of her dreams.

Who would have ever thought such a wretchedly miserable day would become so brilliant?

She lifted her lips at the thought, earning a smile from Lord Whitevale—one that warmed her chilled body from the tips of her soaking toes to the crown of her head.

Then, without warning, he gently plucked the tiara from her hair and turned to the clerk. "Yes, this is it. Will you have this sent to Cranbourne Lodge this very day? Enclose this, will you?" He handed young Hamilton a letter.

The clerk bowed. "Yes, Your Royal Highness—I mean, yes, sir."

"My thanks, Miss Royle. You have made my decision for me," Lord Whitevale said. "I have no doubt this will suit . . . her . . . perfectly."

Her? Who is he speaking of? Utterly confused, Elizabeth peered up at him, waiting for an explanation. But he gave none. Instead he bid her and Anne good afternoon, then abruptly quit the shop and followed his footmen into the dense rain.

"Bertrum," Hamilton, the elder, whispered rather loudly. "Why did you insist on referring to Lord Whitevale as His Royal Highness?"

Bertrum did not bother lowering his voice. His tone told Elizabeth he meant for the ladies to hear his words. "Because that is who he is. I saw his procession arrive two days ago. I was in the front of the crowd and saw him clearly. And here, look at the signet in the wax sealing his letter."

Suddenly Bertrum pressed the letter flat to the glass case and held a small lamp to it before his father could snatch the missive away. "I knew it. Look at it closely. His signature is visible through the foolscap."

"I do apologize, ladies," Hamilton stammered. "I assure you, this is not the way I conduct business. Every purchase is entirely confidential."

Elizabeth didn't care a fig about that. She pinned Bertrum with the gravest of gazes. "Who is he? Please tell me."

Appearing most proud of his sleuthing abilities, Bertrum lifted his chin. "That gentleman, Miss Royle, was none other than Leopold of Saxe-Coburg."

Elizabeth's legs gave out from under her, and she grappled for a nearby chair. "You don't mean . . . Prince Leopold of Saxe-Coburg?"

Bertrum grinned. "Indeed, *I do.*"

Lord, help me now.

Next month, don't miss these exciting new love stories only from Avon Books

Bewitching the Highlander by Lois Greiman

An Avon Romantic Treasure

When Highlander Keelan awakens after a century of magical slumber, his only goal is to recover the Treasure that caused his family's downfall. But Charity is also seeking treasure and when they cross paths, sparks are sure to fly.

The Forever Summer by Suzanne Macpherson

An Avon Contemporary Romance

Lila Abbott is used to the unexpected, but she couldn't have predicted that a woman would drop dead in the supermarket aisle . . . or that her ghost would decide to stick around! Now she has to soothe a cranky spirit, while trying to deny her attraction to said ghost's very sexy—and very alive—ex-husband.

What Isabella Desires by Anne Mallory

An Avon Romance

Marcus, Lord Roth, lives a daring life and knows that love has no place in his future. But when Isabella Willoughby throws herself in the path of danger, Marcus will do anything to protect her life . . . and his heart.

Tempted at Every Turn by Robyn DeHart

An Avon Romance

Willow Mabson is the height of propriety, but all her rules are thrown out when she becomes involved in a murder investigation. Determined to assist Inspector James Sterling, Willow didn't count on this impossible attraction. But how can she develop tender feelings for a man who's doing his best to throw her parents in jail?

REL 0707